Shytown Girls Book 1

Shy-Town Girls

ISBN 978-0-9883471-3-7

Chicago, IL
www.networlding.com

3 8001 00109 3362

Shy
Town
Girls

M. G. Wilson, Jennifer Yih,
Katie Leimkuehler and Kate Clinesmith

Dedication

To all those shy girls who want what every girl
wants—to give love and receive it bravely.

—The Authors

Preface

Because this was truly a collaborative effort with a focus on mentoring young professionals which is a passion of mine, we have chosen to include all of our names on each book. We also decided to put my name first to keep the continuity of this four-part series.

Each book will have a different character's perspective. Additionally, as we found from our early reading audience, they preferred a first-person narrative as they identified with the characters more that way than through a third-person narrative.

This book has been a tremendous project in what I hope will be a very enjoyable book for anyone who reads it. Finally, I want to thank all of my co-authors and wonderful project team for bringing it to life. We could not have done it without each other!

In gratitude,

M. G. Wilson

Chapter One

The leaves were turning and the air was cool, swirling around me as the Chicago wind is famously known to do. Today was the first day of fall and the first day of my new single life.

I was starting a new chapter. A chapter without Charlie, without fear in the back of my mind. I had finally made the choice to let go and allow myself a fresh start. I leaned my head against the window of Charlie's black Land Rover as we slowly made our way through the heavy traffic into the city. I closed my eyes, feeling the hum of the car's engine, becoming lost in the moment.

I need this, I told myself. My heart ached as I thought about all the time and energy I'd put into my relationship with Charlie. In the beginning I had seriously thought he was *the one*. Yeah, I was wrong. And it hadn't taken me long to realize just *how* wrong. I wished it hadn't taken me so long to let him go. Our relationship had its good moments, sure, but not nearly enough of them. If I were to choose a word to describe what I had with Charlie, it was *draining*. But today was the day I would finally muster up the strength to say goodbye to him. I had tried to say goodbye many times before, but today I knew it would be the last time. Today I would actually do it.

With his eyes fixed on the road ahead, I could sense Charlie's serenity behind the wheel. I knew he thought it would only be a matter of time before I'd come back to him. And by "time" he was thinking, oh, maybe an hour or two. But then he didn't take me or anything I said seriously, anyway. He lived in a world where he made all the rules. He put himself before everyone else. He played games with me and everyone he dealt with. But the worst part was, he brought out jealousy and insecurities in me that were beyond anything therapy could resolve. I knew I needed to date a real person, someone who was whole, and who complimented me. I wanted to be a girlfriend, not a shrink. But I'd become addicted to his tricks and yearned for his approval. And he knew I had been under his spell since the day we met.

The first time I ever laid eyes on Charlie, he had just walked into my office with that lazy, sexy stride of his, a lock of ashy blonde hair falling over his forehead. A top male model can make an entrance when he wants to, but he wasn't even trying. His agent had him assigned to my client list for "personal reasons," according to the memo's few details. I had quickly guessed what those "personal reasons" might be, when I looked over his file before our meeting. From his photos I could see he was something special, even for someone in his profession. Working for a modeling agency, I was surrounded by plenty of gorgeous people, but no one's look impressed me as Charlie's had. It wasn't just his gray-blue eyes, chiseled cheeks and strong jaw. It was something about the slightly imperfect way it was all put together. It was something mournful in his expression that made him seem so deep and lonely, just waiting for the right girl to come along. Or the right guy—he was a fashion model, after all—but whatever.

My heart was yet untouched. I'd seen lots of attractive boys before, and if truth be told, at that point I was actually more excited about Charlie from a business standpoint. It'll be groundbreaking for my career if I get to represent this guy, I thought greedily... dollar signs flashing before my eyes. I had no thought of sleeping with him, let alone any future fantasies of domestic bliss.

No, it actually happened the moment he came through the door. I looked up from my desk and our eyes locked. And stayed locked, for way longer than reasonable. I knew then he wasn't going to be just a client. It seemed to happen that way for him, too. He looked at me like a panther contemplating a squab. I was shocked by the force of his impact. I deliberately refrained from shaking hands with him, which is unusual for me. We could hardly speak. Instead we gazed at each other like it was love at first sight. We both started talking at the same time, both stumbling over our words, blushing and tense, both aware of that undeniable pull you feel when you know you need to be close to someone. And it wasn't just words I was stumbling over. In my nervousness I knocked down a little crystal vase on my desk, and he dove for it, saving it from crashing to the ground. As I reached out to take the vase from him, he gave me his hand instead. He set the vase down on my desk, but he kept my hand in his and didn't let go. "I'm *very* pleased to meet you," he said. That was the first time we touched.

That was it. My heart was gone.

To me, his beauty was more striking than anything even Michelangelo could have dreamt of painting.

And, as we know, he had an expert eye for gorgeous guys, too.

"Bobbie, wake up. We're here." Charlie nudged my shoulder. He might have stroked my cheek with his signature touch, but not this time. I think he knew better. He had parked the car in front of a very large three-story Victorian on Dearborn Parkway, but the engine was still running, as if he didn't think we'd be staying. This was it: my first apartment in the city. It was a stately, beautiful old house, overgrown with wisteria vines and ivy. The ornate black iron railing that led to the front door was old and worn, but was polished to a shine and the entire home seemed to sing with history and vintage charm. It was as if the home, like a museum, was inviting you to come in and visit.

"You're sure about this?" Charlie hesitated before unlocking the doors.

I nodded.

His eyes, now grayer than blue and slightly glassy, held a look of disbelief. "I still don't understand what I did to make you want to leave. This is impulsive, irrational."

"I think I forgot my toothbrush in the bathroom," I said, ignoring the comment. Impulsive? Maybe.

Irrational? No. Staying with Charlie as long as I had—*that* was irrational. "You can throw it away," I continued. "I'll buy a new one."

"Bobbie, are you hearing me? Why are you doing this?" His hand gripped the steering wheel, his knuckles white.

I could feel the pressure building up in his hands, and in my chest, like a hundred tons of weight crushing my heart. "Charlie," I said, "I've been in love with you since the minute we met, but it's not right between us. And don't look at me like you're so innocent. You know exactly what I'm talking about!"

"Oh, no!" he threw his head back against the headrest. "*This* again, Bobbie? Jesus."

"You *cheated* on me!" I yelled, suddenly losing any control I thought I had.

"It's ancient history! Fucking hell. I can't believe you're at it again."

"Correction, you mean *you're* at it again. And I'm not an idiot. Let's go," I said, opening the door of the car. "For the record, I hate it when you swear at me."

He grabbed my arm. "Wait. I'm sorry. I keep forgetting how sensitive you are."

I raised my eyebrow, looking at his hand on my arm. He let go.

"I want to be with you, Bobbie," he said. "Even if it doesn't mean living together. I want to give you your space if you need it, but please don't ruin everything we've built together."

Nice words, right? Too bad I'd learned—over and over again—that he was striking a pose like he had done thousands of times before in front of a camera. This time though I wasn't buying it.

It was on the tip of my tongue to tell him that I was sure he was still cheating on me, even though I knew he would deny it. I could have forgiven him once, and I thought I had—but there was something about his attitude that made me think I'd never be able to trust him again. I know. I had tried for a year.

I was too drained to fight. Not now. "I just need to find some independence, Charlie," I said. "And that's not something I can do if I'm living with you. Let's go."

I jumped out of the Land Rover, threw my purse over my shoulder, and ran up the steps to the front door. Charlie got out and began to unload my boxes, thumping them down on the ground, probably hoping to break something. I held down the buzzer with a little more pressure than necessary.

"Who is it?" a voice asked through the intercom.

"Bobbie Bertucci. I'm moving into the bottom floor

apartment with Ivy and Ella."

The front door buzzed and I walked in. Charlie followed, carrying boxes. As I stepped inside the entryway, I did a quick scan and was blown away by the old-style elegance of the building. It smelled like cinnamon and mahogany, and was all lofty vertical lines, tall windows and wide casings, the wood worn, but well-kept. The floors creaked with every step as we walked past a sweeping, grand staircase with a turned banister, and down a short hallway on the main floor beneath a chandelier dripping with real rock crystal drops.

"This is it," I said. *Apartment 1A*, read the sign in gold above the big black-painted door. This was would be my new home, my fresh start. I took a deep breath, knocked, and opened the door. "Hello?" I said. I suddenly felt very shy.

"Bobbie!" The voice, full excitement, called from behind me. Charlie and I both turned to see Meryl's blonde wavy hair bouncing as she flew around the corner from the stairway. I was relieved to see a familiar face in my new surroundings.

"Meryl, hi!" I dropped my bag and embraced her. Her hair smelled like fresh linens and sweet lavender. I had met Meryl outside a lecture hall on the first day of my freshmen year of college, when she had glanced over at my iPod and our bonding over Brazilian music began. She was a grad student working on her thesis. "Oh my *God*," she had exclaimed. "You're into Vanessa da Mata too?" I told her about the trips I had taken to Brazil for Carnival with my eccentric family. She told me about her dreams to dance samba in Rio de Janeiro. I told her about Mangueira, the samba school I had attended that is the oldest of the samba schools and promised to teach her all the moves I knew. I also promised her I would one day go to Rio to Carnival with her. From that moment on, we were friends. Seven years older than me, Meryl was the girl who invited me to all the hottest parties, who bought me alcohol before I was 21, and still managed to inspire me to pull straight A's—like her. She was the big sister I had always wanted. I found out later that she had an enormous trust fund, something you would never have guessed from her modest habits. Only her incredible generosity to one cause after another, especially when it came to helping those younger than herself, gave any hint to how well-off she was. Now, in her early thirties, with her master's degree, Meryl pursued her dream to work as a publisher. With her added love for all things electronic, especially anything with an apple on it, she was quickly becoming a top publisher of digital books in Chicago and beyond. I loved and respected her for so many reasons. If there was anyone who paved her own path, it was Meryl.

"Hi Charles," she said flatly. He gave her a nod. "Bobbie, do you want some help? We have a surprise for you if you want to wait on the boxes."

"Helloooooooo *dolly!*" I heard an unfamiliar voice. Sweeping down the stairs in a China-red silk top and midnight-blue flowing skirt was the beautiful, silver-haired Barbara Shafer. I had never met her before, but Meryl had described her to me—raved about her, really—when she had talked me into moving in. Barbara, who owned the house, was in her mid-70's, but she had an intense vitality and a glow about her that would make her look forever young. As she grabbed me and gave me a big hug and and light kiss on my cheek with her ruby red lips, Charlie slipped out to the car for more boxes. I smiled, blushed and tilted my head down as I did so often when I was truly embarrassed.

"Welcome to your new home, doll face!" Barbara laughed and then smiled with real warmth. "Oh my goodness! You *are* beautiful!" She cupped her hands to my face as if she was examining a marble statue.

"These eyes, they're like—Godiva chocolates. What do you think, Meryl? Milk chocolate or semi-sweet? And this luscious dark hair..." Barbara smelled like rose perfume. She smacked her lips again against my blushing cheek. I knew for sure she had left a bright wet crimson lipstick mark on my face this time. I didn't mind.

"Come, come, honey," she said, hooking my arm in hers. "I have a surprise for you. Drop those bags. Forget those boxes. Worry about them later." As she led me back down the hallway to the stairs, she leaned in and whispered, "Who is that dashing young man you brought with you?"

"Oh, he's just the lying cheat who stomped on my heart," I said lightly. "Otherwise known as my boyfriend, Charlie."

"Oh, wow. Hang on to that one," she winked. I think she was being sarcastic or she didn't hear me. We started up the stairs, with Meryl following and Charlie lingering somewhere behind us.

"Barbara, wouldn't you rather take the elevator?" Meryl asked.

"I've got two legs that I'd best use while I still can, honey," Barbara said. For my benefit she explained, "Meryl installed an elevator for me last year after I took a little spill. I'm not quite as nimble as I used to be, baby, and I did an uncanny impersonation of Humpty Dumpty on this staircase here. Except Humpty Dumpty broke more than just his hip, didn't he?" she added drolly.

"That's awful," I said. "Are you okay now?" The image of her tumbling down the steep wooden stairs was frightening.

"Well, they couldn't put Humpty back together again, but they could for me. Pretty good job, too, wouldn't you say?" She swiveled her hips suggestively as she climbed the steps in front of me. "I want you to make yourself comfortable here, Bobbie. This is your home now. So, you're down on the first floor with Ivy and Ella. I have the flat on the second floor, and Meryl is here on the top floor in her 'ivory tower,' as we call it."

By now we were on the third floor landing, but we didn't stop there. I admired Barbara's stamina as we climbed a total of three very long flights of stairs. These old Victorian buildings were tall.

"Now, I want this house to be filled with nothing but love and harmony," Barbara said. "This is very important to me. Mutual respect, openness, honest communication. If you have any problem whatsoever, you come straight to me and we will take care of it!"

Finally we came to another smaller landing. We had reached what I hoped was the top. "You hear me, honey?" Barbara said earnestly. "We are a family, and we take care of each other. And I will expect you to obey the house rules at all times. No men, no alcohol... unless you share!" Was she kidding? I'm sure she was. While I blushed for the umpteenth time, she continued, "And here we are! Ready? One, two, three..." she pushed open a big, black worn iron door. A large gust of wind almost blew me back down the stairs.

The first thing I saw, when I was able to get my hair smoothed down and out of my face, was a tiny blue-black ball of fur, hurtling toward me and wagging furiously.

"This is Due, who usually needs to be shushed when he first meets someone. But clearly he knows you're family. I don't even have to tell him to be quiet!" Barbara tried to temper the onrush of friendly puppy. "I got him from that amazing shelter that Oprah contributed big bucks to—PAWS. Due is a terrier-poodle mix of some sort. This no-kill shelter is the cat's meow," she winked, "pun intended. He usually barks when he first meets someone to make sure they are friendly, but he already realizes you're one of us."

"Due! Sit!" ordered Barbara, and Due sat, still wagging.

"Wow! I can't believe he understood that! He's adorable!" The moment I knelt down to pet him, Due licked my hand and then rolled over onto his back, begging me with brown, soulful eyes to scratch his speckled belly. "With a welcome like this," I laughed, "how can I not feel at home?"

After that last surprise, I found myself finally relaxing, not feeling the anxiety pangs that flowed through me during the drive over. I took a deep breath, lifted my head up and smiled. I suddenly felt eager to see what would happen next.

Chapter Two

Leaning over the railing that ran around the rooftop garden, I was awestruck by the fabulous view—the expanse of Lake Michigan and the incredible skyline that defines the windy city. Comfy woven wicker chairs and chaises with kelly green cushions were scattered around the terrace. The garden itself was enchanted, with deep, greenish-purple vines running up and over Tuscan red brick walls and tangled around dozens of multi-colored flower pots filled with perennial pink asters and stunning clumps of Purple Dome asters amid yellow, purple, bronze and white chrysanthemums.

Barbara shared all this with me as she explained, "It's important for everyone in the house to *know* the flowers and to make sure they're watered and cared for correctly."

My eyes were drawn to the big table spread with a red checkered cloth and covered with assorted crackers, cheeses, sliced baguettes, olives, and prosciutto with melon.

Two women who looked to be in their mid-twenties came sauntering through the roof-doorway, carrying trays of glasses, a bottle of champagne, and a glistening pitcher of orange juice. I knew from looking at their Facebook photos that these were my new roommates, Ivy and Ella.

"Bobbie!" Ivy plopped her tray down on the table, rattling the champagne glasses as she ran up to me and introduced herself. Ivy was petite, with ivory skin and high, prominent cheekbones. But it was her mischievous energy, and her big, gorgeous blue eyes— so striking in contrast with her long black hair—that would keep me sneaking looks at her. As a modeling agent, I'm always drawn to unusual beauty, and she had it—in spades. Automatically I reached out to shake hands with her, but she quickly drew her hand back and grabbed me in a hug instead. "We're friends now," she said decisively. "None of that hand-shaking crap!" she said emphatically.

"It's great to meet you, Ivy," I said, hoping what she said was true. Would we be friends—or merely roommates? It's not like you can just decide these things. Making friends post-college was never as easy as it was in school.

Ella, on the other hand, came off as cool, but I had a hunch she was just shy, like me. Her straight, silky brown hair just touched her lean, muscular shoulders. She was as pretty as Ivy, but with a delicate simplicity and a cat-like expression. I noticed how graceful her movements were as she relinquished the pitcher to Barbara, then wiped her slender hands on a cloth, and walked over to join us. She gave me a hug too, if somewhat less exuberantly than the others.

"You are now an official resident of 721 Dearborn," Ella proclaimed in a quiet, ironically official voice. "Welcome."

"Thank-you," I said. I put my hand over my heart and looked at each of them in turn. "I'm so glad to be here." And I meant it.

Barbara, who was pouring drinks, called, "I'll drink to that!"

Now that the four of us were all together, the energy level on the terrace suddenly tripled.

Ivy handed me a mimosa. "Cheers, roomie!" she said, tapping my glass.

"Welcome to the family!" Barbara raised a glass to me. Meryl and Ella followed suit.

"Wow, this is amazing, you guys," I said. "Thank

you so much for everything. Barbara, this house, this rooftop, it's just so magical. And this drink isn't bad, either." I looked at Barbara and back at the girls again, my eyes almost teared up in gratitude. It was an emotional day, and I tried to get a grip. I did not want to lose it in front of these people I barely knew. And I did not want to lose it in front of Charlie, who had just emerged from the stairwell.

As usual, when Charlie appeared, the setting suddenly took on the glamorous aura of a Vogue photo shoot. With his slouchy, elegant sexiness, Charlie's manner seemed off-hand, almost sleepy, while at the same time revved and dangerous. All the women present, from the oldest to the youngest, responded— arching, lifting, purring. Even Meryl, who didn't like Charlie, was not unmoved.

The spell was shattered when Due emerged from the corner at full speed, barking ferociously. "Oh Due, be quiet!" Barbara attempted to hush the little puppy who skidded to a stop and stood valiantly, and very vocally, between Barbara and Charlie. "He's my champion," she said. "He barks when he first meets someone to make sure they are friendly. With that statement she looked sternly at him and said, "Due! He's Bobbie's friend." With that, the little dog stopped barking and came forward to sniff Charlie's ankles.

Charlie looked down at Due but made no move toward the pup. I pulled back my shoulders and forced a smile. I felt tired and stiff, but the little dog's attitude when greeting me versus how he barked at Charlie made me feel a bit more cheerful. I hoped my low energy didn't show. I wanted the girls to know how much I appreciated the warm welcome, and I wanted Charlie to think I was nothing but excited and thrilled to be starting my new life. Without *him*.

"Everyone," I said, "This is my boyfriend, Charlie. He's helping me move in." The word *boyfriend* rolled almost unnaturally off my tongue. *Ex-boyfriend* is what I meant to say. But the moment had passed.

"Well, hello handsome," Ivy twirled over to him, offering him a girlish handshake and a blazing smile. I had a hunch she wasn't on her first mimosa.

"Hi Charlie," Ella said with a little wave.

Barbara and Meryl uncovered the trays. "Eat, honey!" Barbara commanded me. "You too, Charlie." I was too overwhelmed to eat anything, but didn't want to be rude, so I got up and made myself a plate. I caught myself as I was about to ask Charlie if he wanted me to fix him one, too.

Even though I appreciated the gesture of the party,

I felt uneasy with all the attention focused on me, the questions hanging over me and Charlie. But everyone seemed so nice. Then it hit me: these women and this place were now my life.

"So, Bobbie, how long have you two been dating?" Ivy asked with a cheek full of food.

I glanced at Charlie. "Two years," he said before I could answer.

"That's cool. You guys are *such* a hot couple."

"Thanks Ivy," I said. "But officially, you know, Charlie is the pretty one. He's the model. I'm just his agent."

"So that's like—your girlfriend is your boss!" Ivy slurred.

"No. The client is the boss, not the agent," Meryl said.

"Are you sure? Then how come the agent can fire the client?"

"The client can fire the agent too. Right, Bobbie?" asked Ivy. "It works both ways. Doesn't it?"

"It's been great meeting you all," Charlie said. "But I think I'll go bring the rest of those boxes in and leave you girls to it."

I wanted to reach for him, not wanting him to leave me yet, but he'd already turned his back. I sat down with my plate and proceeded to swig back my first mimosa. I didn't have much of an appetite, but the drink went down fast and easy.

"Ok girls, another roast—I mean, toast—to the newest member of our family." Meryl held her glass high. "The beautiful Bobbie Bertucci, long time friend of mine, and one of the greatest girls I know. You're going to fit right in here, Bobbie, and we're happy we can be a part of this new chapter in your life!"

The ladies whooped and hollered, clearly eager to embrace any excuse to celebrate. All except Ella, who stood there quietly, lowering her long dark eyelashes over her smooth cheeks, studying her drink. Meryl had warned me that she would be more reserved than the others.

"And now, it's time for the cake!" Barbara announced.

"There's cake, too?" I held the back of my hand to my forehead and pretended to swoon. The mimosa had loosened me up a little. "You're right, Meryl," I said. "I won't be able to fit into my skinny jeans, but I'll fit in here!"

Ivy put her hands on her hips and pouted. "Are you sayin' we're fat?"

"Not us. Just you," Ella smiled like a pirate.

"Who wants coffee?" Barbara asked.

"I do," Ella said.

"Only if you've got Bailey's," Ivy replied.

"Down girl," Ella said, lightly slapping Ivy's arm.

"What? It's *Sunday*."

"Barbara," I said, "can I help you in any way?"

"You just keep your cute butt in that seat," Barbara hollered. We could hear her singing all the way to the door of her apartment.

I was on my second mimosa when Barbara came back with a giant cake, homemade whipped cream, and a bowl of mixed berries. "My famous pound cake!" she announced with a flourish. "Bon appetite, doll faces! The coffee will be ready in a sec."

"I hate to be rude," I said, "but will you all excuse me for a minute so I can say goodbye to Charlie?"

"Go, go!" They all waved at me, nodding.

"Do your thing!" Ivy said.

I sprinted down the steps. All my boxes were inside the apartment, and I found Charlie outside. He slammed the tailgate of his Land Rover and turned to me.

"That's the last of it," he said, all business, as he wiped his hands on his dark grey jeans. "You going to be okay?"

I nodded. Something seemed to have taken hold of my throat.

"Don't cry, Bobbie." Charlie took my shoulders in his hands and leaned forward to press his forehead into mine. God, he could be so sweet sometimes. I couldn't remember the last time I'd felt so connected to him, but I knew it was an illusion. I knew his sweetness was an act, and I knew better than to let my emotions get the best of me. I was making a bold move here. This was the right decision. The only decision. I pulled my shoulders back and sucked up the tears. My heart was sinking again, and I found it hard to swallow.

"You don't have to do this," he said, not for the first time.

But I do, I thought. I *do* need to do this. Doesn't he *get* that? His selfishness angered me.

Charlie wrapped his hands around the back of my neck and gazed into my eyes. He poured out all the power of that expensive, soulful expression, as if a photographer was aiming a camera on him. *Give it all you got, Chance.* That was his professional name. Chance. Oh, yes, just to look at him, no one could deny he was intensely gorgeous. A sadly stunning character. Undeniable and vulnerable beneath his gaze. Smoldering even. But his fingers felt ice cold to the touch on the warmth of my neck. I shivered.

"Thank you for helping me move," I said, pulling away. "I'll see you at the office."

"Is that how it's going to be now, Bobbie? You treating me like a client?"

"That's what you are, right?" I murmured. "A client."

His eyes grew cold and he set his mouth in the hard expression I had come to know so well. It was the same expression he'd worn in the French cigarette advertisement, the same one he always turned on me when he was frustrated or angry. "Figure out what you really want, Bobbie," he said. "Because otherwise you'll never be satisfied. I'm not going to hang around and be some knight in shining armor for you every time you create a crisis for yourself."

"I think you should go now," I said, feeling my face grow hot. He leaned in to kiss me, but I turned my cheek.

He threw up his hands. "Fine—have it *your* way, babe," he said. "See you around."

The last thing I would remember in this moment were my own words stuck in my head like a bad song playing over and over again—*you asked for this. Now go find something better.*

Chapter Three

After being wined and dined in celebration of my moving in, it was time to start unpacking my colossal stack of boxes. I walked around the quiet apartment, my hands in my pockets, taking it in. The tall windows, the wide, intricate woodwork, high ceilings, the elegant vintage light fixtures. It was wonderful. My new roommates, Ivy and Ella, were still upstairs chatting with Barbara and Meryl. I was grateful for the moment alone, a moment to breathe.

The living room was large, with a gorgeous old fireplace, a fantastic bay window, a big L-shaped couch, a papasan chair, and a big screen TV. I saw a few movie cases lying on the floor. A boxed set of *Friends* that was clearly bootlegged from China. *How I Met Your Mother, Modern Family, Entourage, Mad Men...*I was liking what I saw. There was a rack of *Happy Madison* movies, *Saturday Night Live* starring Will Ferrell, Chris Farley, Adam Sandler, David Spade. Wow, Meryl was right! After browsing their entertainment collection, Ivy and Ella seemed like long lost friends.

Still reading titles, I almost tripped on a pair of shoes. Jeffrey Campbell, I noted. Great choice. Photos of Ivy and Ella, along with their friends and family, covered the mantel. Some of them had engraved frames with cheesy sayings like *No Road Is Long With Good Company.* If this worked out, maybe my photo would be in one of these frames soon. It was hard to envision.

There were two bathrooms in the apartment, one updated double-vanity bathroom and a smaller one that Meryl had said would be mine. The little bathroom was cold and sterile, but when I flicked on the light and saw the ancient claw-foot tub, the painted vanilla woodwork and cream tile, I could see it had potential. Hopefully with some TLC I could make it work. I figured Meryl would support me in financing some redecorating since she was the trust fund baby swimming in more money than she knew what to do with. Most of the work she had done so far had been to make sure the place was safe for Barbara, while creating a space that was fabulously chic and classic.

My new room was smaller than the one I was used to, and I had downgraded from a king bed to a double.

I looked at the mattress, fighting the urge to feel sorry for myself. I hadn't slept alone in a year. Well, at least I had a view. I walked over to the window, parted the sheers, and looked out. Beyond a profusion of overgrown rose bushes, a couple was walking down the street, hand in hand.

"I bought you a body pillow to spoon at night," Meryl said from behind me.

I jumped. "Jesus, you scared me! Did you seriously?"

"No," she chuckled, sitting down on the bed.

"Bobbie, I'm going to be honest with you. I love you, but you've been in and out of relationships since college and even before that. You are so ambitious, beautiful, brilliant—for God's sake, you speak three languages! But you don't know how to say no to a relationship, especially a new one that *appears* right, but comes with all kinds of warning signs right in front of your face. You get too caught up in the guy to see them. This is your chance to be single and be on your own. You need this."

I said ruefully. "I think I'm crazy sometimes. When I was saying goodbye to Charlie I wanted to slap him across the face, but then again, I wanted to hold him and never let go."

"It's not Charlie you want to hold on to. It's the idea

of him. Bobbie. This is your chance to be independent. From everything you've told me, Charlie is a jackass. You don't want to hang onto *that*, do you?"

"Only sometimes, but hey—I'm making progress," I said in my own defense.

"Yes, you are definitely making progress. You're here, aren't you? You're going to love living with Ivy and Ella. I'm only two flights up, and Barbara is like the mother I never had," she added with a smile.

"Barbara is amazing, and she's so beautiful!" I remarked. I was already feeling better just switching the subject and picturing Barbara's whimsical presence. "Actually, so are Ivy and Ella. It's refreshing to be around people that don't know how beautiful they are and leave room for sincerity. It's foreign to me. Jesus, how pathetic is that?" I hadn't had the chance to vent in awhile. It felt good to verbalize that I hated the shallowness that absorbed my life. At last, I was surrounded by real people.

"Barbara was a legs model back in the day," Meryl said, "which was basically the equivalent of a Victoria's Secret model today."

"I knew it!" I said reassuring my sense of professional expertise.

"So, anything else I can do to help you settle in?"

she asked, generous as always. "I'm at your disposal. I can even run out and pick up anything you might have forgotten."

"No, I just need some time to adjust. Hey, Ivy and Ella, they're okay with this? Me moving in? The two of them seem so close. I feel a little—intrusive."

Meryl gave me one of her big motherly hugs, winked at me and said, "Stop worrying, Bobbie. Everything will be okay if you want it to be. Don't forget, you live in the city now!" Meryl glided into the living room and started taking hats off the coat rack and trying them on. She was an old soul and somewhat of the big sister I never had. "The big nights of watching TV with your boyfriend and going to bed early are over! Especially with these girls," she laughed. "You have no idea who you've got yourself into."

"Did I hear drinks tonight?" Ivy shouted from the bathroom. Through the open door I could see her sitting on top of the sink, plucking her eyebrows, her face two inches away from the mirror.

"I was just filling Bobbie in on the fact that living with you two clowns comes with perks—like never staying in evenings. Unless it's with a Redbox and bottle of wine."

"Correction! Bottles!" Ivy emphasized.

"Or ice cream and Oreos, depending on the day." I couldn't remember the last time I'd touched Oreos or ice cream, or anything processed for that matter.

"Why don't we go out tonight, then?" I suggested. "It'll be my treat! We can do dinner and drinks...or just drinks. Ya?"

I looked at Meryl's and Ivy's eager faces, "I could use a night out to get my mind off douchebag mcgee." I said referring to Charlie. I also knew a few drinks would ease any awkwardness and speed the bonding process.

"Yes!" Ivy jumped off the counter and did a little dance, jazz hands, black hair swaying.

"I'm in!" Ella shouted from her bedroom. Apparently this apartment had thin walls. Meryl gave me a nod and another one of her winks.

I whispered, "I told you, progress."

For the next hour we did what girls do best: getting ready. The iPod dock was blaring through the apartment. Ella and Ivy exchanged and shared with me every beauty tool and accessory known to womankind. They were more like sisters than best friends, arguing and insulting each other one moment, laughing and joking the next.

"Ella, where the hell did you put the blow dryer?"

Chapter Three

I heard Ivy shouting.

"Wherever you left it! Can I borrow your blue dress?"

"Yeah, if I can wear the tan Jeffrey Campbells!"

I slipped into my classic red dress and set my suede pumps on the toilet seat. Alone in my bathroom, listening to Ella and Ivy giggling together over their double vanity, I couldn't help but wonder they were thinking about me. I was unsure of the impression I was making. I remained quiet in my bathroom, feeling more awkward than usual. What if three *was* a crowd? It probably would be, even in a big bathroom like that. I laughed in the mirror at my patheticness. I'm a grown woman, feeling sorry for myself, thinking like the new kid in the High School cafeteria.

I curled my hair, drew black cat eyes, put on red lipstick to match my dress, and added a splash of Coco Chanel. My mother's voice always ran through my head when I was getting ready to go out for the evening. *"Classic will always trump trendy, Roberta. Find your scent and stick to it. Don't you ever forget how the women of Roma dress, the women of Paris walk, and the immaculate perfection of the Austrians. A little vanity goes a long way, Roberta. Scusi per la mia vanita."*

"I was thinking we could go to Hugo's. What do you think?" I stood at the doorway to their bathroom, the first one ready.

"Oh Bobbie, that dress rocks!" Ivy blurted. Ella gave a nod of approval. Then she added, "And Ella and I LOVE Hugo's!"

"Hugo's is big on fish, aren't they?" Ella asked, pouting at herself in the mirror as she dabbed color on her lips. But it's up to *you* tonight, Bobbie." She hadn't said much to me all day. I studied her face for some signal of emotion, some sign of what was going on inside. She looked at me expressionlessly, then looked away. Our eye contact, or lack of it, felt awkward. Did she not like fish? Or was it me she found distasteful?

"Knock, knock!" sang out Meryl. "Shall we?" She popped her head in the door. We grabbed our coats and locked up the apartment.

"Have fun, dollies! Toodaloo!" Barbara's voice echoed down the stairway.

"She's not coming?" I asked.

"She's got a date with Rock Hudson," Meryl said. "She loves old movies."

"Wait—" Ivy frowned. "Wasn't he gay?"

Ella gave herself one last look in the hall mirror. "Like she would even care!"

Chapter Three

I laughed and called out goodbye to my new landlady. I was already taken by her contagious warmth. I smiled as I walked out the front door into the cold.

Chapter Four

"Welcome ladies. How many?" The hostess at Hugo's greeted us with a big smile on her face, her hair crusty from hair spray, over-applied. Yikes.

"Party of four," said Meryl sweetly.

"It's going to be a bit of a wait. Can we interest you in a drink at the bar?"

"How long's the wait for a table?" Meryl asked as she put on her professional face.

"About twenty minutes, but I'll see what we can do for you Ms. Harrington," the hostess beamed. I realized that Meryl was a regular here, wining and dining her clients. She was glowing with pride as the Hugo's hostess did all she could to accommodate us. Hugo's held a number of Meryl's charity events, resulting in significant donations to various foundations. Unlike the philanthropic Meryl, I never was the charitable type, maybe because I was too focused keeping my life together I didn't have the energy to look out for anyone else.

Ivy then stepped up, "Is Jacob Shields dining tonight? He's a close friend. If not, I know he'd be happy to give us his table. Should I give him call?"

"Oh, Mr. Shields. That shouldn't be necessary," the hostess's attitude shifted. She looked at Ivy with eyes of wonder and then leafed through her reservations list, stopping cold. She looked up with a toothy smile. "Mr. Shield's cancelled this morning as he said he was going out of town!"

"Perfected," Ivy lit up with self satisfaction. With that she swooped up four menus, whisked us over to a great four-seater overlooking Rush Street and daintily passed the menus.

"What was *that*?" I asked Ivy.

"What?" Ivy shrugged. "Jacob's one of my bosses at the PR firm, and he owns like half the city," she said. "I knew he was out of town."

"Really?" said Ella with an arched brow. In my line of work, I had certainly met a quite a few divas who knew how to secure the VIP treatment and I was proud to say one of them was my new roommate.

As we'd walked to our table, I noticed all eyes were on our foursome. That's when I realized I was traveling with a highly attractive entourage. Ella was rocking some Jeffrey Campbell boots, making her legs look like they went on for days. Meryl wore pale pink lace and carried a Birkin bag; and Ivy was stunning in a black satin dress that glistened in the dim lighting. I knew my trademark red dress flattered my figure, and my confidence escalated from our runway walk from the front door to our table. Being with these girls helped keep my shyness at bay. I waved the bartender over, he must not have been a day over twenty-one. He smiled cutely, "What can I get you ladies?"

"St. Germaine's and soda for me," I said. "What are you girls drinking? Tonight's on me."

"Oh no, Bobbie. You're not buying!" Meryl tapped my hand three times. This was her signal for me to back down.

"Nothing for me. I'm not drinking," Ella said.

"Oh, come on Ella, just one drink," I insisted. She looked at me with a chilly expression, and I instantly regretted my words.

But then she shrugged her shoulders. "Okay," she said. "One won't kill me. "Pinot Grigio, okay?"

I smiled with relief.

"Holy hot bartender!" Ivy shouted. "I triple dog dare you to leave your number on a napkin." I did.

Our conversation finally began to flow like the

drinks I continued to order. We all had much more in common than I had previously guessed. I discovered Ella had been a dancer for majority of her life, explaining her poise. I assumed she was the kind of person that expressed themselves without words. I happily informed her that we weren't so different. I'd been a dancer for fifteen years but I had only stuck with my ballet career as long as I did only because my mother had insisted that it gave me grace. Ella's passionate side came out as she told the stories of her past performances. She had danced in the Joffrey *Nutcracker* and still took classes at Hubbard Street. Ella urged me to come with her some time. She was much more talkative after her first cocktail, and although I had no desire ever to put my feet back into a pair of ballet shoes, I thought it might be worthwhile if it helped us bond.

Ivy went to the bathroom three times while we were at the table. She said she had a nervous bladder. I wasn't sure what that meant, but her anxious energy was contagious. I couldn't help but laugh at her whimsical personality. She was drinking rum and Coke—and not Diet Coke. I wondered where all the calories went in her slim figure.

The jazzy music of the restaurant put me at ease

along with the hum of voices and clinking forks and knives. The four of us decided to order several appetizers instead of main entrees. We picked, sipped, and chatted. I hadn't been surrounded by so many girls in some time. I was on my third drink when I found myself revealing a side of me I hadn't seen in awhile.

"I might just have another drink!" Ella said. "Easy tiger," Ivy said. "Let's relocate to Luxe Bar for drinks. My friend Danny is working and that means free drinks. Wahoo!"

"You mean Danny Danny? Your slampiece?" Ella snorted.

"He wishes!" Ivy threw on her coat.

I was surprised I wasn't tired, like I usually felt after a few drinks, but it was hard not to be energized around the girls. Ivy took my hand and danced into the entrance of Luxe bar, the lights flashing, music bumping, and crowd lively. I felt alive.

"Vodka soda!" Ella yelped down the bar, looking back and me and giggling. She ordered one of the lowest calorie drinks that always got the job done. Nice work. The bartender handed her the drink, shooting her a seductive wink. She blushed.

"Bartender just checked you out!" I informed Ella.

She shushed me, embarrassed.

"That's the spirit!" Ivy slapped Ella's back, which caused her glass to slip from her fingertips, slide down the bar with a life of its own and spilling all over a curly-haired man wearing a linen sport coat.

"What the—" he sputtered turning around to see the culprit.

Ella tried to say something, but nothing was coming out. She stood like a deer in the headlights.

"I'm so sorry," I said, apologizing for her. Ivy was holding her stomach, cackling. Meryl was trying not to laugh, grabbing napkins.

"Let us buy you a drink," I said as a peace offering. Making everyone happy had always been my role and now it was my job—I was a professional. I knew this guy couldn't turn down four pretty women. We officially had the attention of everyone around the bar. I felt like I should have been embarrassed by my friends, but I wasn't.

"Is your friend okay?" Tacky Linen Sport Coat Guy asked me, nodding at Ella, who still stood frozen. Ivy pinched her butt. She quickly snapped back to reality.

"I'm really sorry," she stammered. "Do you need more napkins?"

"It's okay. It's not the end of the world," he smiled

at her reassuringly. "You know about dry cleaners, right? I'm Steven." He reached his hand out to Ella and gazed at her a little too long. Oh great, I thought, the perfect opportunity for Linen Sport Coat Guy to hit on her. I was eager to hear which line he would try. I would have bet that nine out of the ten men standing around the bar were wishing she would spill a drink on them.

Ella introduced him to Meryl and Ivy, evidently hoping to pawn him off on one of them.

"Nice to meet you, Steven in linen," Ivy said. I chuckled. Ivy continued, "Don't you know it's autumn now?"

"Are you saying my coat isn't stylish? It's just because I don't have a gorgeous girl like you to dress me," Steven said. *Oh, gag me!*

"Yeah okay buddy. I prefer big boys who can dress themselves," Ivy spoke down to him like he was dog. With a grin, she sipped her drink. The girls chuckled, and the server brought over Steven's peace offering drink.

"Thank you for this," he said. "Maybe you girls can spill on me again some other time."

I raised my eyebrows. Could he be any more tacky? Is single life always this entertaining? Ella groaned as we turned to make our way through the crowd. "I really hope he didn't mean that the way it sounded," she said in a low voice.

Linen Sport Coat retreated to his booth where he and his two friends kept sneaking glances at us. If I were to guess right, I'd say his friends were financial analysts, and tacky sport coat guy was working for an insurance company. A server brought over a bottle of champagne. "From the men at the booth." I gave them a wave, praying they wouldn't come over.

Ivy poked at her phone. "Ugh. How do I delete this stupid horoscope app!?"

I turned to the group a little drunk and asked, "What's your sign?"

Ivy looked at me under her eyelashes, "Really? That's like a question someone would ask on E-harmony."

"How would you know what's on E-harmony, loser?" Ella giggled at herself.

I continued, "I used to date this crazy guy in college named Francis who used to tell me my daily horoscope, I even let him read my cards once."

"What you dated a psychic? Don't tell me you're into that zodiac hocus pocus. Ella is too. Bunch of B.S. if you ask me," Ivy shouted over the noise.

"This was during Bobbie's hippie, save the world, no showering, backpack Europe days. Francis had dreadlocks too!" Meryl gave me a look.

"What he was totally hot, for a hippie!" I defended.

"Meryl, you're a Cancer, like me. We're supposed to come off as shy, yet honest. When we are uncomfortable, like crabs we retreat into our respective shells."

Ivy leaned in, her interest roused.

"It was weird because Francis was pretty spot on. It threw me off when he told me that my favorite numbers were three and seven, which is true."

"What else did he say?"

"Supposedly Cancer the crab is ruled by the mystery of the moon. We're loaded with contradictions and constantly working for stability, whether it's emotionally, romantically, or financially. We're jealous, moody, insecure. But we're close to our family and friends. So, there you have it, me in a crab shell."

Meryl laughed and said, "Bobbie, that *is* spot on."

"I know—creepy isn't it?" I said.

Ivy raised an eyebrow. "What about me? My birthday is April Fool's Day. I know I'm an Aries, but that's about it. Do you know anything about Aries?"

"Ah, Aries, if I remember right…your element is fire," I said.

"No surprise there," mumbled Ella.

I dug into the memories of my 'organic' days when Francis would waft in with the newest aromatherapy trend and a memo of my daily horoscope. He was always telling me to get in touch with my inner crab— and to lose the shell.

"Let me check," I said. I snatched Ivy's phone and began reading the app. "Okay, Aries. Your life pursuit is the thrill of the moment. You're always enthusiastic, and you like to be a leader. You tend to trust your gut before your thoughts, which can be troublesome if you find yourself in the middle of some kind of drama. You retreat easily in order to think about the aftermath of your actions. But you're the life of the party!" I winked. "I added that last part myself."

Everyone laughed.

Meryl chimed in. "I have the same app on my phone. I know I'm a Cancer and strangely, it's usually pretty accurate! It says I'm strong and bold on the outside, but sensitive on the inside." She smiled.

I nodded. "I agree with that, Meryl," I teased her. I had a flashback to a midnight phone call from Meryl a few years back. She had called off an engagement to her fiancé. To this day, I never really understood why. She had refused to share the details. "But seriously, you are strong about what you believe in. You don't back down. Especially, when it comes to taking care of others, or defending the underdog. You are a true lioness." I was drunk.

Ella sat quietly listening, her hands crossed neatly on her lap. I wasn't sure if she was having fun.

"What about you Ella? When's your birthday?" I asked.

"I'm a Pisces," she said proudly.

"Pisces, that's the fish. Do you know much about Pisces?"

"Some," she answered, not giving me much to work with. I looked at Ivy's phone app for more information.

"Well, am I right to say that Pisces are intuitive, imaginative, kind, and sensitive?" I asked.

She nodded in agreement. "I think so."

"On the dark side, Pisces are a bit secretive, are they not?"

"True," she confirmed, reaching for her drink. I didn't want to push her any more, as my intuition was telling me Ella felt awkward when she was put on the spot. I could relate.

I suddenly realized as I looked up at the clock against the main wall of the bar that it was almost midnight. I still had not prepped for my meetings the next day and for once I didn't seem to mind. No one in the office would believe me if I told them I was hungover. *When did I become so lame?* I also realized that I had not checked my phone all night. In fact, I had not thought about Charlie once.

The four of us walked home that night chatting back and forth the whole way. It felt like we had been together like this before. Even Ella looked more at ease. After brushing my teeth, washing my face and drinking two large glasses of water in hopes to avoid any hangover, I fell asleep almost instantly. Right before I slipped into a deep sleep I had one lingering thought—what if I wouldn't miss Charlie...at all?

Chapter Five

I woke up the next morning almost forgetting where I was. As reality sank in, my stomach lurched when Charlie's face came to mind. I guess last night's hopeful optimism was only temporary.

I stormed into the office, late as usual. Punctuality was something I needed to work on. The phones were ringing, my head pounding, and people hurrying this way and that. Striding down the white florescent-lit hallway like a starved model on the runway was the infamous Wolfgang Lutz, my boss and the director of Fordham Model Agency. I quickly turned the corner to avoid a confrontation regarding my tardiness.

"Morning, Miss Bertucci," chirped the new British secretary for agents as I scurried into my office. "There's a memo on your desk."

"Great, thanks," I said, and shut the door. I sat down at my desk, logged into my desktop computer, and organized my work for the day. The first hour of the morning was grueling. Not from work, but from my own head-tripping. Every time I heard footsteps tapping past my door, my stomach dropped out of paranoia that it was going to be Charlie: his gorgeous face that I loved to hate; his long, lean body; that hypnotic stare.

I was happy to see an e-mail awaiting me from my younger brother Adrian. He was off gallivanting in Europe, supposedly attending school in Rome at John Cabot University. From the random messages I received from him, I suspected he was actually spending more time exploring shot bars in Paris and being one with nature in Amsterdam than studying. It made me miss my own adventurous days abroad and my old carefree attitude toward life.

Ciao ciao, sister!

Guess where I just got back from? Yes, that's correct, LONDON baby! Wish you were here. You should plan a trip this winter. I know you've been dying to get back to Rome ever since you graduated. Just imagine: we can walk the streets of Trastevere, drink wine on the steps of Piazza Trilussa, Piazza Navona, and Trevi by night! And eat gelato till we puke. How bad do you want to slap me right now? Anyway, I'm backpacking Prague this coming weekend so don't freak if I don't respond.

Did you break up with that toolbag/Zoolander model guy Charlie yet? Tell Mom and Dad I said what's up. Peace big sister!

With love from Roma, your baby bro,

-Adrian

Attached was a picture of Adriane with my friends Devin and Beau whom I had met on a backpacking trip to Europe. They were standing in front of the London eye with giant pints of Magner's cider. I envied my brother's freedom. Every time he contacted me, it made me want to quit Fordham and escape this superficial world. Below his email were two emails from Charlie. I couldn't bring myself to open them.

I picked up the memo that Wolfe had left on my desk.

BRAZILIAN MODEL: MARIA MURARI, BAHIA BRASIL, AGE: 19, ENGLISH: NONE,

AGENT: ROBERTA BERTUCCI

English: *None*. Great another one, I thought. Now the only jobs I could send her out on were one's I could attend and be the translator. They didn't pay me enough for the overtime I put in trying to bridge language gaps. I began to poke around online, looking for some English classes.

Working at a modeling agency had its benefits:

over-the-top galas, the constant tide of beautiful people, and of course, the very latest fashions. But the majority of models you see in magazines are insecure, unstable people with massive ego issues lost in perpetual identity crisis. And other kinds of crises: expired visas, heroin addiction, one or two pounds of weight gain. Sometimes I felt more like a therapist than an agent. I kept a large poster on my office wall of a triangle diagram. At its three points, the labels read, "Intelligent," "Good Looking," and "Emotionally Stable." In the middle of the triangle, it says "Pick Two." I usually classified myself as lacking in emotional stability, but looked like Dr. Phil in comparison to the train wrecks that waltzed into my office.

Feeling claustrophobic, I took off my scarf, stacked the papers on my desk, and had the urge to throw everything out the window and burn down my office. *Breathe. Breathe.* My anxiety was escalating. Coffee? Or not enough coffee?

"Knock, knock," I heard the voice outside my door. I glanced up with a sigh of relief to see Oliver's big green eyes.

"Olly..." I sighed. He floated across the room making it feel fuller and lighter at the same time.

"Miss Booger Bertucci." He walked in and set a cup

of coffee on my desk.

"Mmm...Hazelnut?"

"Pumpkin spice," he winked.

Oliver wore his standard outfit of faded jeans, combat boots, and a dark green jacket that complimented his forest green eyes. "And how are you on this wonderful morning?" he asked his voice smooth.

"Stressed. My new model from Bahia doesn't speak a lick of English, so I'm trying to get her into some classes. If I can do that, it'll really improve her portfolio. It's amazing that these models get recruited, brought to the U.S., and don't even know the language. Anyway, life is much better now that you're here. What's up?"

He flashed his crooked smile, always sweetly contagious. "Well...as far as the models go," he said, "that's what you're here for. To hold their pretty hands and make them stars on the cover of *Vogue.*" Olly smoothed the air as he envisioned the *Vogue* cover page.

"You're looking rather flowy today," I complimented sarcastically. Oliver needed a haircut and, more so, needed me to remind him. His chestnut locks were beginning to curl on the ends. He looked a bit like

Michelangelo's David. I always liked the way his cow lick flipped over revealing his forehead.

"What—didn't you hear?" he said. "I've decided to pursue my male-modeling career. You know, I think it's *really* my calling." He posed like one of the many male models I managed, moving his hips in isolation like a samba dancer. "All nat-u-ral Bobbie," he sang, smoothing his hair with the blade of his hand.

I covered my mouth and laughed at his ridiculousness.

"Good lord. If you keep that up, I promise you I will vomit," I stared at his hips.

"What? Am I not doing it right?" he continued posing.

"Wow. Maybe you should ditch the photography and coach my models," I laughed. "Okay, please stop, right now. Stop. You are not normal."

He finished with an exaggerated pelvic thrust and threw himself down in the chair beside my desk. "Yeah, I'll stick with taking the photos, thank you very much. Behind the camera is where it's at," he said with a sigh, slouching back and picking something from his tooth.

"Everything all right in there?" I asked watching him dig for gold in his molar.

"Scone bits from earlier, all good. So...how are the new *roomies* and mansion in the *Gold Coast* working out?"

"So far, so good. I hear that sarcastic tone, watch it smart ass. Anyway, it's definitely going to be weird getting used to, but I think I'm going to warm to living downtown. The house is incredible. You need to come by and see it, maybe take some photos. It's gorgeous, vintage almost, and they're making a few renovations—it's going to be amazing. And as far as the girls, they are mostly really great."

"Mostly?" He raised a brow.

"Yeah."

"You mean *most* of the girls are great, or all of them are *mostly* great—"

"No, they're great. All of them."

"But you said—" he teased.

"Olly!" I threatened to smack him. "I *just* moved in. It's too soon to say. And why do you say *Gold Coast* like it's a bad thing?"

"Come to my hood, Wicker Park, this weekend," he said. "Leave your lipstick, perfumes, and designer crap at home and see how the other half lives. I'll buy you some low calorie beer," he teased. "My friend Sam's band is playing. They're kind of a Mumford and Sons meets Blink-182 meets the Beatles kind of thing."

"Blink-182...God. Do you remember that concert?"

"Yeah, when Travis came down from the sky like a drummer-god."

We relived the moment together. "Do you still have that t-shirt I got you?" I asked.

"Somewhere, definitely." He sighed. "Please don't remind me of those days."

"You mean high school? Mr. Prom King."

"Pfft. It was a fluke. Someone rigged the votes!"

"Oliver, are you blushing?" I called him out. "You know you were *totally* that artsy fartsy mysterious guy all the girls made up stories about," I laughed.

"Bullshit!" he threw his head back and laughed.

"Yep, don't deny it," I pointed at him. "I remember one of the best rumors was when you got back from London and people were saying that you joined a band and had been on tour with—"

"I *know*. And I hear I was actually with my family on a Christmas holiday. Although, I did

bring my guitar with me on that trip, so maybe you don't know *everything* about me."

"It's all about style points, Olly. Ew, that leather jacket with the weird design on the back you used to wear..."

Chapter Five

"You know, I'm beginning to regret bringing you coffee," he said rubbing his temples. "I mean, I know I wasn't as cool as Bobbi-snobby. Forgive me if I didn't import all my fabrics from Italy and make all my own clothes by hand. You weird ass."

"You didn't complain about the jacket I made for you. On second thought, weren't you wearing that when you lost your virginity? Huh, weird. You're welcome." I patted myself on the back.

"Touche, I owe you my manhood." He pressed his palms together and bowed. "You are a goddess. I worship you."

"Of course you do. And you know, Olly, I really do appreciate the over-roasted coffee," I said sipping and cringing. "So, when's your next shoot?"

"I've got to go pick up my spiffy new camera and shoot some French chicks at Trump Tower today." He clapped and rubbed his hands togther. I loved that he was more excited about his new camera than being swarmed by European models.

"Ooh, French chicks, exciting," I mimicked his starry-eyed expression, clapping and rubbing my hands. "That should make your day."

"No, my day was made when I walked in and saw you."

"Ahh..."

The sincere look he flashed me sucked the air out of me. Something mysterious was going on behind those deep green eyes. It was an expression he'd turned on me before, but only rarely, a secret weapon if you will. It always made me feel naked when he looked at me like that, but I knew it would only be fleeting. To cover my confusion, I made another wisecrack. He returned with one of his own, and we both laughed.

"Bobbie, can we talk? Alone?" A new voice interrupted playtime. Deep and resonant.

My stomach flip-flopped at the sight of Charlie's face in the doorway. I wasn't sure how long he'd been standing there, eavesdropping. The mood in my office had deflated like a dead balloon. The morning had just turned into an episode of *Days of Our Lives.* Oliver threw me a glance, pushed up from the chair, and stuck out his hand.

"Charlie, how are ya?"

Charlie ignored Oliver's hand, hardly feigning to look at him.

"Alrighty then, Booger," Oliver said, "I'll catch you later."

"Have fun at the shoot today, Olly," I called after him. "Thanks for the coffee!"

Charlie took Olly's seat, which was probably still warm and infused with the scent of Old Spice.

"Bye Booger," he mocked Oliver, "Really Bobbie?" he asked condescendingly. "Are you going to trail that puppy around forever?"

I wanted to slap him, "You're an asshole Charlie."

"That's why you love me," he replied, crossing his legs.

"And *disturbed*." I hated him right now. If he wasn't one of our top earners at the agency, I would have fired his ass a long time ago.

"How's the sorority house treating you?" he asked not evening pretending he cared. His ego was swallowing up the air in the room. I took off my blazer.

"Everything is good. What do you need Charles?" I asked professionally. I crossed my hands, leaned back in my chair, then sat back up to rest my elbows on the desk. *Quit moving.* He stood up and sat on my desk, folding his arms and looking down on me. I watched the steam rise out of the mouth of my coffee cup. *Keep it professional. Stop fidgeting.* I was about ready to stand up and walk out.

"I went to that hand-model casting call you sent me to," he said. "By god, there were some ugly people there! Anyway, they turned me down."

"Oh? Well, thanks for informing me." I said trying to pretend I wasn't pleased he'd been rejected.

"I guess I don't have pretty enough hands," he lifted his hands and examined them in the sunlight blazing through my windows. I looked into his eyes for the first time since he had walked into the room. They were ice blue. His concrete stare caused the area from my lungs to my stomach to quiver. He didn't blink. He knew what he was doing, teasing my emotions.

I stood slowly, lightheaded from skipping breakfast, and made my way to the window to draw the blinds that caused his eyes to glow.

I tried to be professionally optimistic, "I'm sorry to hear that Charlie, but you didn't want to get into commercial modeling anyway, remember? I think you should just stick to the higher end, private sector gigs, in my professional opinion."

I looked out the window, staring into an office that occupied the skyscraper across the street. I wondered what was going on in that office. It was probably a financial group housing analysts in their cubicles, praying the markets were having a good day.

I felt Charlie's breath on my neck.

I turned and put my hand on his chest. "Stop."

"What? It'll be like the old days," he said, his voice

soft, sweet and persuasive. "The good old days..." He leaned in to kiss me.

"Charlie, stop," I whispered. But it was half-hearted, and he knew it.

He kissed my top lip, then my bottom lip. I closed my eyes, feeling weak in my ankles, my stomach flipping, dizzy. I should've eaten breakfast.

I had spent only one night away from him, and I felt like I was kissing him for the first time. I pulled away quickly, but it was too late. He knew he had me. I broke away.

I grabbed a binder from the shelf above my desk and slammed it down on my desk.

"I'm going to make some calls," I said in a very businesslike voice. "I'll let you know when your next shoot is. I can't do this right now, so please go."

"Good girl," he slapped the desk. He skipped to the door and just before turning the handle he pulled out an envelope from his coat pocket tossing it on my desk. "You have yourself a wonderful day Miss Bertucci," he said, pointing at me. The door slammed behind him causing me to jump. The chandelier above my desk jangled. I touched my lips as they burned from his kiss.

Chapter Six

I opened the envelope Charlie had dropped on my desk. Inside was a note with a key taped to the back. The note said, *The door is always open, waiting for you to come back to me.*

Dammit! I ripped off the key and threw it across the room. It pinged and panged against some ugly and useless decor Wolfe's designer had left in the corner.

My phone buzzed, and I snatched it up. It was a text from Meryl. *Lunch? I'm feeling Thai Food.*

My response: *Please, Star of Siam, Illinois Avenue, 12:30*

I beat Meryl to the restaurant and sat alone, waiting. My memories began to get the best of me as I sat and sifted through moments Charlie and I had spent together the past few years. Nervously, I drummed my fingers on the table. I felt as sick as I did at the moment I had first learned what had happened. *Why the hell is it taking so long for her to bring me a glass of water?* My heart dropped to my stomach when I pictured Charlie and me lying together on my suede couch, him asleep, his face angelic and peaceful, so incredibly beautiful, as always. I remember I had wanted to kiss him, but knew that I'd wake him if I did. He didn't like it when I did that.

While I was gazing down at him so adoringly, I saw his phone light up on the coffee table. *3 a.m.* Who could possibly be texting him at this drunken hour of the night? Of course, his psychotic ex-girlfriend! The one he'd dated when he was a freshman in college and who hated me so strongly that I wouldn't be surprised if she spent her Saturday nights poking needles into a voodoo doll she'd made of me.

"Happy Belated Birthday Charlie" read her pathetic text. Idly, I began scrolling through his messages. There were other texts from her. Quite a lot of them. And quite a lot of texts from other women as well. I scrolled and scrolled and scrolled…It was like numbers running down the walls in the Matrix, only it was a neverending list of stripper names like Brandi, Alissa, Sara, Natalia, Claudia, Kaci, Stacey, Bethany, Tiffany… followed by stripper-like conversations such as "come on over" "Can I see your dorm room tonight?" "I rented us a movie" and "What's taking so long?"

Freshman year in college? Really, Charlie? As if it wasn't enough, competing with 5'10" models, let's add in a few eighteen-year-olds! Hopefully they're at least that old.

I felt my face getting hot and a sort of tunnel vision activating. I could hear the blood pumping through my ears. Disgusted at the sight of him, lying there with one lock of dirty-gold hair curled down over his forehead, I disentangled myself and slowly got up off the couch. I nearly lost my balance, but without any hesitation, I cocked my arm back as far as it would go, and harder than baseball hall-of-famer Nolan Ryan could throw a pitch, I chucked Charlie's stupid iPhone at his stupid face.

He yelped, leaping off the couch in a panic, grabbing his forehead.

"What the *hell*?"

"Get out, Charlie," I said. "Get out *now*!"

He looked at me as if I'd lost my mind. In a way, I had.

"Get out Charlie, I read your texts." I turned around, slowly walked up the spiral staircase and locked myself in my bedroom. I heard him follow me slowly up the stairs, one step at a time, open the front door, and SLAM! The waitress dropped a cup on the table causing the water to splash everywhere, "Water?" I snapped out of it and stared at the Asian girl thinking she'd be much prettier if she smiled more. My phone buzzed, Meryl:

"Hey, where are you?" I asked.

"Bobbie, something came up, I can't make it I'm so sorry, explain later," she rushed.

"No problem, want me to drop anything off for you?"

"No, I'm okay. I have a surprise lunch with an author that's just in town for the day. Are you okay?" sincerity in her voice.

"Yes, I'm fine. Charlie made a surprise visit to the office. I let him kiss my, like an idiot."

"Oh no, you know what, I'm coming. I'll cancel."

"Meryl, no. I'll be fine." I begged.

"You sure?" her voice worried. We said our goodbyes. I did not mind a moment alone, sometimes talking about my relationship made things worse. My mother always told me the more attention you give to something the more it grows, good or bad.

"Excuse me, can I get the Pad Khee Mao to go please?"

I walked out of the restaurant and decided to take my time getting back to work. I made my way out onto the street and took a left. I never walked down this way. A crowd of tourists walked straight at me. I was about to get swallowed in the little sea of foreigners.

I looked up to see something flipping around in the air. A flyer? Scrap paper? It hit the ground over my left shoulder; it was a $20 dollar bill! I stopped immediately and looked behind me to see from whose unlucky pocket this has fallen. There's a woman with a purse and a man with his hands in his pocket. The man starts crossing the street on a diagonal; the women keeps walking forward. Why is everyone walking so fast? By now two people have bumped into me since I'd stopped dead in my tracks mid-sidewalk. I'm confused: is it his or is it hers or is it neither? All I know is that someone in a ten foot radius dropped twenty bucks on the ground. I turned and walked away leaving the twenty dollar bill on the ground for some other sweet soul to find. I looked back to see if anyone had picked it up and saw a man on his cell phone spot it. He actually went out of his way to walk *around* it like it was some steaming pile of dog doo doo. I laughed and continued walking.

I came across an old used bookstore called *After Words.* I decided to go in because Meryl was always talking about books and authors. To be honest, I didn't even really like to read. Most books were too long, with boring characters and tedious story-lines. I always lost interest within the first thirty pages.

A woman wearing a beret greeted me. She was carrying on an impassioned conversation with the man behind the counter. Apparently she thought *Anna Karenina* was *way* better than *A Tale of Two Cities*.

"What's your favorite book?" the woman turned and asked me.

"*The Great Gatsby*," I said impulsively.

"Really?" she looked at me without smiling. "Why?"

"Because a) it's a classic and b) it was the only book assigned in high school that I actually read—because it was the shortest. The rest of the books I looked up in SparkNotes."

The woman rolled her eyes and shook her head. "Can I help you with something?" she said.

"Yeah, where's your legal section located?" I asked.

"You looking for something like Contracts for Dummies?" she studied me.

"No, more like books for law students," I affirmed.

"Isle six," she mumbled studying my wardrobe.

I walked over to the "Legal" section of the isles and skimmed through a few case books. The only things I ever read for pleasure were magazines, Calvin and

Hobbs comic books, and majority, dissenting, and concurring opinions from Supreme Court cases. I spotted an old man behind the front desk. He looked like a scrawny version of Santa Claus.

"Excuse me. How much are these case books?" He looked up at me as if he never even saw me come in. I figured he was writing the next *War and Peace* behind that little desk of his, judging by the length of that beard.

"Fifteen dollars each," he croaked.

"I'll give you twenty for both of these," I bargained, holding up a First Amendment and Due Process case book.

"Meh," he nodded and waved me over. I smiled on the inside. I loved it when I got my way.

"Case books, huh?" he asked insincerely. "Law student?"

"No, I was a political science undergraduate. I guess I just like to read justified arguments," I said honestly.

"I was a law professor for years. You're young. Go live your life. Law schools aren't going anywhere," he responded bitterly, seemingly ignoring my response. I wondered if he sensed that I had impulsively decided not to go to law school in my senior year of college.

Today, his comments were reaffirming my decision.

"Twenty bucks," he barked, "I misplaced twenty bucks today. That's what happens with old age."

I looked at him, puzzled, "Thanks," I said, and walked out.

Chapter Seven

There are four distinct seasons in Chicago, and each brings a new personality to the city. Folks say there is no greater adventure than the thrill of discovering what the Windy City will blow in one day and out the next. Several weeks had passed since I mustered the strength to leave Charlie and move in with the girls. Aside from that one moment of weakness on the first day, I kept my promise to myself. I wasn't giving in to my weakness for Charlie, no matter what he did to convince me otherwise. Not being one to admit he'd been dumped, Charlie remained moderately persistent, keeping up a steady presence in my life, reminding me of his existence whenever possible. Fortunately we were both swamped with work and too busy to play games.

The office was silent, the way I preferred it. I was working late tonight, trying to get caught up. But when my phone buzzed three times in a row, I decided to answer. *Can't someone take a hint?*

"Yeah?" I snapped.

"Roberta, honey, how *are* you?"

"I'm good mom, busy at work..." I sighed. I loved her dearly, but I was in no mood to have a conversation with my over-analytical psychologist of a mother.

"Well, I was just checking in to make sure you're taking the move-out move-in situation okay."

"Yes, mother, everything is working out fine," I said. "How are *you?*"

"Well, my shoulder's bothering me again, but other than that...so, how's the boyfriend?"

"His name is Charlie and not good. I'm slowly ending things with him."

"It seems a bit unorthodox to be *slowly* ending something, doesn't it? I can understand things can seem complicated, but in my day things were pretty black and white: you go steady or you don't." When I stayed silent, she pushed, "So what's going on with you, Bobbie? I think there's something you're not sharing with me."

"It's different nowadays, Mom. I really don't want to get into it. My feelings and attitudes towards love are a little...exhausted."

"Roberta, attitudes represent generalizations

about phenomena based upon extrapolations from previous experiences—"

Here she goes.

"—and usually take the form of cognitive generalizations, so yes, your attitude toward love is most definitely what I would call askew...In order to have a *tabula rasa* effect on your life, you'd have to literally be reborn and that is not happening, so I suggest you start creating new and better experiences for yourself, because that will determine the outcome of your future. Find yourself a man who demonstrates consistency. That's my best advice, honey."

"Okay, Mom, thank you," I said, trying to keep my cool. I wanted this conversation to end. Unfortunately, it didn't. Not without another ten minutes of analysis.

7:30 p.m. on the dot. I cleaned up my desk, logged off my computer, packed my bag, and locked up my office. On the way out, I heard pounding, slamming, and a few swear words from the copy and blueprint room.

"Hello? Is everything okay?" I looked in the room, but didn't see anyone.

"Oh, hi," a high voice stuttered. "I didn't know anyone was here." She was crouched on the floor, short boyish bleached blonde hair, bright big bug-eyes, and pink little lips. I noticed she was trying, unsuccessfully, to cram photo paper into the copy machine.

"Do you need some help?" I asked. "You do know that paper doesn't go in there, right?"

"Oh yeah, I knew that," she lied with a big smile as she stood up, turning completely pink, obviously embarrassed. "I'm trying to make copies of these photos by..." she read the memo.

"Oliver...Price, no wait— Oliver Prince."

"Olly's photos?" I took the blue prints and began sifting through them. Excellent work, as usual. One photo caught my eye, and I pulled it out of the stack. A handsome older man embracing an older woman who held his face tenderly in her hands.

I sometimes forgot what an amazing photographer Olly was, with his uncanny ability to capture real life moments, evoking even more emotion from a two-dimensional photograph than even reality exposed. His photos hinted at someone much deeper than the lighthearted Olly I knew.

"I'm Lilly. I've seen you in and out of the office," she said, and extended her hand for a shake. "I'm an intern."

"How long have you been interning here?" I asked, surprised. I'd never noticed her before.

"All summer," she replied. *Woops.* "And I'll be here for the rest of the fall." She leaned in close to me. "You smell really good."

She was a quirky one, with her wild hair and the way she was blatantly invading my personal space, something that just didn't happen at Fordham Agency. Here, if you got too close to another body, you ran the risk of getting slapped silly. She kept touching her hair out of nervousness. Her body was lanky and awkward, as if she hadn't grown into it yet. I figured she must have been about nineteen. Her sporadic, ungraceful movements were strangely amusing.

"Thanks. It's Coco Chanel."

She smiled, nodded, and seemed to be taking mental notes. "Expensive, huh?"

"Don't worry about the photos," I said. "The photographer is a friend of mine, and he's pretty easy-going. I'm sure you can pick up where you left off tomorrow." I watched her relax, and I handed her back the photos. "Nice to meet you," I said, and walked out. I made my way to the elevator and hit the star for the lobby floor.

As I walked through the big glass and marble lobby, I could almost taste the smell of Lysol on my lips. "Hey, wait up!" I looked back to see Lilly the intern, her heels clacking on the marble floor, her knees buckled inward as she jogged along attempting to catch up with me. She really was awkward and reminded me of some tropical bird.

"I figured we could share a cab or walk or something," she said breathlessly, obviously trying to be my friend.

"Sure," I said, though I really wasn't thrilled with the idea. I had been looking forward to a few minutes of mindless meditation.

We walked out and made our way towards Michigan Avenue. "So, you must love working here at Fordham," she said. "I go to DePaul. I'm a design student, and I was really lucky to get this internship. You must be over the moon with *your* job. Being an agent and everything."

"Sure, if you love working with snobby, insecure people who lack depth, take this industry way too seriously, and you're okay with depriving yourself of all real knowledge in life because your head is so filled with meaningless trivia. If you want nothing more than to be surrounded by starving beauties, then yes, this is your heaven."

"Oh wow, that was honest," she said. "So...why do you do it, then?"

"After college I lived in Italy for awhile and I made some connections in the fashion industry. Then I helped a friend from Milan get into modeling here in Chicago when I got back, and one thing led to another...I found out I'm good at it. I'm really into contract law, for one thing. I'm good at connecting people with other people..." *At least in my professional life*, I thought. In my personal life, I felt insecure and inept. "And I'm a good advocate for my clients," I went on. "I tend to get them good terms, you know? Because I don't mind a fight. I stand up for people."

At least for *other* people I do, anyway, I thought. For myself, when confronted with any kind of conflict, I tended to curl up in my shell like the crab I was. "And the design aspect of the industry is cool, too. Working with some of the great artists, photographers, designers...I'm not that artistic or anything myself, but I really appreciate beautiful things, and the people who create them."

"Well, I want to be behind the camera, not in front of it."

"I guess that's the best place to be," I said, thinking of how happy Oliver seemed to be, taking photos for a living.

As if she had been reading my mind, Lilly said,

"I really like that guy Oliver's photos. How old is he, anyway? He's so *cute*. I feel like he should be one of the models."

"Olly?" Her comment surprised me. I thought about his silly strut in my office. "He's not really the model type," I said. I pictured him, how he looked that morning, when his shirt pulled out of his belt as he lifted his arms above his head and rolled his hips in an exaggerated figure-eight. His moves weren't bad, I reflected, and the glimpse of his bare torso above his low-slung jeans had showed a surprisingly hard-looking plane of muscle. But *cute?* Sure, Olly was cute, with his open, curious expression, his ready, crooked smile. That's exactly what he was, *cute*. Not devastating, mysterious, dangerous...

Like Charlie.

We were almost to the Chicago Red Line stop when Lilly said she was going to hop on the EL and take it up to Rogers Park. I decided to walk home from there, enjoying the hustle and bustle of the city by night and the vigorous exercise. Under Ella's influence, I had taken up dancing again, going with her a couple times a week to classes—jazz, hip-hop, and ballet. Now that my mother wasn't making me go, I found I actually enjoyed my dance classes. It was all very familiar, yet new and exciting. And it was fun to go with Ella, who was clearly in her element, looking like a Barbie in a beigey-pink tank and tights, and a slouchy fisherman's sweater she took off after warm-ups to reveal a muscular, slender athlete's body.

We tried to get Ivy to come with us, but so far no success. "I only dance with a drink in my hand," Ivy said. Barbara and Meryl wanted to try a class, but they always had something going on—charity work, family and friends, Barbara's weekly swim, Meryl's writing workshops. They kept busy.

Chapter Eight

"Hello. Anyone home?" I called as I unlocked the door of my flat. As I walked into the beautiful three-story building, I realized how quickly it had come to be *home*. I saw Barbara's light on in her living room, but the lower level looked dark and quiet. I switched on the light, and I felt a glow of happiness. *Home*. It was definitely feeling like home. If only the feeling wasn't accompanied by a corresponding loneliness. It was great living here with the girls, but I missed being in a relationship. I missed *love*. I missed a sense of true purpose in my life. *Purpose,* was a bit ambiguous, more like I was obsessed with putting all my energy into a worthless relationship.

In my room, I slid out of my shoes, putting them neatly back in the box. I unzipped my dress and grabbed a pair of boxers, along with a big white sweater. My feet were freezing, so I slipped on my knit socks. I was dying for a warm drink. Nothing sounded better than hot chocolate and Bailey's.

That's when I heard banging on my ceiling. Thump, thump, thump. "Hello?" Barbara's theatrical voice called down the stairway.

I ran to the door. "Barbara, it's me, Bobbie. The other girls are gone," I hollered up to her.

"Come up for pie!" she suggested, and I heard Due bark, as if to second the offer. It was one I couldn't refuse.

We chatted a little bit about the weather, which had been wonderful—bracing and cool. Barbara told me about some of her and Meryl's ideas for fixing up the old house. Paint colors, refinishing the floors in the entry hall. Ordinarily I love to talk decorating, but tonight I failed to add much to the flow of creative ideas.

"You're playing with your food, Bobbie," she said finally. "You look lost in thought. Or completely exhausted. What's bothering you, dolly? Is it the pie?" She smiled endearingly as she sat across from me at the kitchen table. Due rested on his own little footstool, following the conversation intently. Or was it the pie he was so avidly focused on? He was a curious animal, his eyes with a human-like personality behind them.

"This pie happens to be some of the best I've had,"

I said honestly. "Ever."

"From scratch too," she said. "I make it from the seasonal Wisconsin Honey-crisp apples."

"No," I assured her, "the pie is fantastic. Thank you. It's just that..." I rested my head on my hand. I found it hard to open up.

"It's good to put your thoughts into words, honey bee," she said.

"I don't know where to start. I don't really know how I got to where I am right now."

"Where is that?" she asked encouragingly.

"I feel so unsatisfied. I also feel ungrateful for being so unhappy. I truly have nothing to be complaining about. I really do like my job—even if I complain about it often. I also have a crazy but great family, friends, good health, and a roof over my head. An amazing roof at that! I love it here. Yet, I am so unhappy sometimes," I confessed. "I just don't know why...well actually, yes, I *do* know. I feel so pathetic saying this, but I think I realized that I've been going about this whole 'love' situation all wrong..."

Barbara laughed to herself. "I'll tell you one thing honey, love is not a *situation*."

"What do you mean?" I asked.

"Love, love, love, one of the most wonderful

mysteries of the world—isn't it?" She smiled and stirred honey into her tea.

"Mystery is right. I don't think I even know what love is. I *thought* I did. But I have learned that I don't."

She looked at me thoughtfully, sipping her tea.

"Did you love your husband, Barbara?" I noticed I didn't see any photos around her apartment of the two of them together.

"Oh yes, very much so," she said.

"How did you know it was real?"

"Real?" She frowned at the word. "Love is not a choice, Bobbie baby. Love takes no work to maintain or to gain. The real choice, the real work lies in the friendship and in sustaining the integrity...the purity of it." She stood and crossed the room to an antique cabinet and opened a drawer. She pulled out an envelope and handed me a photo.

"This is my dear Donald. What a handsome man, isn't he?" she asked.

I nodded. "He is." And he was, with his chiseled jawline, prominent nose, and clear eyes fixed upon something just beyond the photographer. Perhaps it was Barbara herself he'd been looking at. He looked like a man you could count on, someone you could trust to be there when you needed him. *Like Olly is for me*, I thought.

"He was my best friend," she said.

"He's stunning, Barbara," I confirmed.

"Oh yes, didn't I get lucky? My best friend happened to be the most handsome man I knew. Well, I guess you could say I had many handsome beaux, but Donald... he was neither rich, nor poor, but his mind was pure. The way he looked at me..." she paused, reliving a moment long past. "You'll recognize the man you're meant to be with one day by the way he looks at you, Bobbie baby."

Listening to her talk about her late husband with such pride and confidence raised conflicting feelings in me. Envy. Hopefulness. And worry, that it would never happen for me. But also faith—there was a conviction deep down inside me that I hung onto. Believed in. *I,* too, would find what I was yearning for.

"Bobbie, do you know anything about *Eros, Philia, and Agape*?" she asked.

I shook my head. "I mean, yeah, I know the words, I've heard of...well, Eros. He's like the god of love, right?"

"The Greeks were genius people, Bobbie. They faced the mysteries of life head-on, asking questions and doubting the norms. And all this reflecting uncovered the same treasures we still seek today. I wouldn't expect you, or most anyone else for that matter, to know how to identify love—because you're right, you *don't* know what it is. But you, with your knowledge of other languages, have a head start. Because the English language deprives us, doesn't it? It leaves us very confused about what this ambiguous term "love" means."

"True," I said. "Very confused!"

"The Greeks broke it down into three categories. The first stage of love they called *Eros*. Eros is the passions and intense desire you feel for someone, or even some*thing*. Plato said it's the deeply embedded desire to seek the beauty of another individual. When you find something that captures you, it reminds you that true beauty exists in the world. That's a very powerful thing. It's no wonder it consumes us."

I thought of Charlie's beauty, how seductive it was, even when I could see right through it to the vain shallow core.

'He who loves the beautiful is called a lover because he partakes of it,'" she quoted. "Falling in love is loving the space in between you and whatever it is you find beautiful. It's not the individual himself you fall in love with, it is what he provokes from you. Do you understand, Bobbie baby?"

I nodded, but I questioned myself. *Did I understand?* It seemed to me Barbara was talking in riddles or maybe there was something stronger in her tea.

She picked up a glass cup that was sitting on her kitchen table. "Now take this glass, for instance. How beautiful is this? Italian-made, excellent design, hand-blown. It probably took hours of passionate work. Do you think it's beautiful, Bobbie?" she asked.

"Yes, it's very beautiful."

Barbara held it above her head and with great might, threw the glass to the floor, causing it to shatter into a dozen pieces. I was shocked. How crazy was this lady?

She looked at me and smirked. "Do you still think the glass I was holding a second ago is beautiful?"

Shocked and confused I uttered, "Uh—I guess. Yes, I did believe it was beautiful."

"Exactly my point, Bobbie, it wasn't the glass that you loved. It was the feelings it evoked from you. Good news. There are many glasses in the world, of all shapes, sizes, and colors. That is *Eros*."

I felt more confused than ever.

She slapped her hands on the top of her thighs. "Next time you come visit me, we'll talk about the second stage of love, *Philia.*"

"Great," I said. I wondered what she'd destroy to illustrate *that!*

We said good-night and I walked down the stairs. I kept thinking about Charlie's face, and Barbara throwing that glass, breaking it into pieces. I could not figure out what she was trying to say to me, but I had to admit I sometimes had the urge to smash that incredible beauty that was Charlie, see him shatter into a million irreplaceable parts.

But what if it wasn't Charlie at all? What if it wasn't really Charlie who aroused the thrill of passion within me? What if it was all in *me*, like Barbara said? He was just the beautiful container of those passions for me. It seemed cold and callous to reduce a person to a mere vessel for my own inner life. And yet, that's what I'd been doing with Charlie since day one. Back in the beginning I had expected him to hold all my cherished desires and dreams. Now he was the repository of all my deepest disappointment and anger.

I reminded myself that, according to Barbara, my lesson in love was by no means finished. Maybe I wasn't supposed to have it all figured out just yet.

Chapter Nine

Ella and Ivy had just gotten home. "There she is!" Ella called when I walked in the door.

"Bobbie, do you want to join us for a nightcap?" Ivy asked, waving a bottle of red wine.

"Sure, why not?" I chuckled and went to sit down on the couch.

"No, not here, up, up!" Ella exclaimed. "To the rooooof!"

Ivy pointed towards the door, doing a little dance. She handed the bottle to Ella and then presented me with her back. "Unzip me, will you? I'm going to change real quick. I've been dreaming about putting on my sweatpants all day."

As I unzipped the back of her dress, the price tag popped out.

"Ivy, you still have the price tag on this," I informed her.

"I know, I left it on in case I wanted to return it.

Turns out I like it. I was complimented nine times tonight. I kept count. So I'm keeping it—thanks!" She fluttered into her bedroom to change, and I decided to follow her example.

After we'd all changed into warmer clothing, we made our way up the stairwell. Ella jiggled the handle on the big door at the top of the stairs, and it creaked open. A rush of cold air flooded through the crack of the door.

"Brrr," I said.

"Ivy, you've got the blankets, right?" Ella asked.

"And the wine!" she yelped. "Should be drinking brandy in this weather."

"Shhhhhhh, be quiet. We don't want to wake up Barbara and Meryl!"

For a moment it was dark, with only the city lights twinkling in the distance. Then Ella flipped the light switch, and Snap! Pop! Fizz! On came rows of hanging white lights, round bulbs larger than Christmas lights, instantly warming the surroundings. My mouth fell open at the luminous beauty. I had never before seen the roof by night.

"This is amazing!" I looked around at the garden of vines and dried flowers that twinkled like a fairyland.

"It's our little slice of heaven," Ella said. I felt

honored, as if they were letting me into their private world.

"More like our little cup of vino," Ivy said, handing me a glass. "It gets better. Check this out." She turned a knob near the railing and flames came shooting out of a large cylinder bowl surrounded by chairs.

"What? An electric bonfire? Where am I?" I laughed in shock.

"Well, our trust fund baby, Meryl, decided to upgrade this place when she moved in, with Barbara's permission, of course," Ella said.

"Meryl takes pride in fixing things," I said, "on so many levels." I knew this well; she had helped me out a number of times in college when I was a freshman and she was finishing her thesis. Meryl got me through that first year.

Ella poured her glass, and I admired her grace, her slender limbs and athletic movements showing her dancer's training.

"How was your day?" I asked, the warmth of the fire pit heating my feet.

"Just another day in a cubicle in corporate America," Ella said.

"Same," Ivy said flatly. "Except the cubicle. I've been running around like a headless chicken. We have this huge event coming up and my boss is freaking. How about you?"

"I just had an interesting conversation with Barbara before I came downstairs. She's so intelligent."

"Barbara, of course!" Ivy said.

"She's like a modern day Athena meets Ghandi meets Grace Kelly." Ella sipped her wine.

"Her husband was a philosophy professor at Northwestern," Ivy said. "I guess he was a genius."

"I think she might be a genius as well," I said. "She just defined 'love' to me according to the ancient Greeks!"

"Ah—*Eros, Philia, and Agape*?" Ella sang out.

"Yeah!" I laughed. "How did you know?"

"She's constantly preaching that love philosophy to us," Ivy said, rolling her eyes. "As if we don't know what love is. Ha!"

"I mean, it's cool," said Ella. "She's really got some great insight. But…" She gave a shrug.

Was I the only one of the three of us who found this intellectual approach to love intriguing? For the first time, I was thinking of love beyond desire, lust, and falling into that giant web of problems you find yourself unable to escape in a crippling relationship…

"What's *your* love situation these days, Bobbie?"

Ella asked. "Meryl told us about your history with you and model boy, but I'm guessing that's over?"

Over? The word hit me hard. Suddenly I missed Charlie terribly. His warm body in bed at night. The way he listened to me so intently when I vented about work. There was an understanding between us. And more often than not, he would take my side whenever I complained. Whereas Oliver, who also worked in the industry and knew exactly what I was going through. He would usually tell me to suck it up, stop complaining, and be grateful for what I had. As I would do for him the days he was ready to turn his back on Fordham. At least we were in it together.

"Well," I said, "Barbara just got finished telling me that love isn't a *situation*...I don't know, it's so hard to say it's *over*. We've had a long and complicated relationship, and we're still working together. It's been hard just to end it with him cold turkey. I guess me moving in here was a way to ease out of it."

"Ease out of it?" Ivy said, giving me a skeptical glance.

"I know, I guess that sounds pathetic...it's hard to explain." I wanted to end this conversation. I felt offended, and hurt that they didn't seem to get how hard this was for me. Of course they didn't care about me and my wretched relationship. "Let's talk about something else."

"No, no," Ivy said. "We're interested in you. You're holding back on us."

"I don't want to be," I said.

"Explain then," Ella insisted.

"Yeah. Tell us what's going on."

They were pushy tonight. I wrapped the plush blanket more snugly around my shoulders and played with my toes through my socks.

"Do you mind?" Ivy asked. She took a box of cigarettes out of her purse and lit one up.

"Ivy! No smoking on the roof!" Ella said sternly. "And what the hell are you doing? You don't smoke!"

"A cigarette once in a while isn't the end of the world," Ivy smiled devilishly. She offered me one and I shook my head. "Okay," she said. "So what's the story?"

"Well, I started dating Charlie when I got the job at Fordham Agency."

"Right. So it's totally a work thing, huh?"

"Yes. Most definitely. So, we had been dating for awhile, not really exclusively, but he wanted to take the next step. His lease was ending, and he wanted to move in with me. I was thrilled, but sort of shocked that he wanted to take that step, because he wasn't even introducing me as his girlfriend yet. But of course I said okay. Then about a week before he was supposed to move in, I found out he was cheating on me. Long story short, I let him move in, and one year later, here I am."

"Wow," Ivy blurted. "He cheated on you? Just goes to show, some guys won't be satisfied with *anything*."

I hated telling them about this, in fact, I hated telling anyone about it. I was embarrassed about him and my entire relationship. I liked my business staying mine and I was not ready for the opinions and judgments that came along with sharing my relationship drama.

"Shit happens," Ella said.

Ivy stubbed out her cigarette. "Is there anymore wine in that bottle?" she asked.

That was it?

"So, do you think I was stupid for not dumping him right then and there?" I asked. "When I found the texts?"

Ivy shrugged a shoulder. "You said you two weren't really exclusive at the time. I mean, I used to cheat on my boyfriends all the time," she said. "Less complicated that way."

"You're crazy," said Ella. "How is that less complicated?"

"I know it wasn't right. But I think it was a way for me to end things when I wanted to be free."

What? I couldn't believe Ivy's detached attitude. I had *never* cheated. I didn't think it was possible for me to cheat. My conscience would always get the best of me.

"Bobbie, I think it's selfless of you to forgive him," Ella said.

"No one's perfect. You gave him a chance and now you can go on with no regrets, because you tried," Ivy said.

No judgment? Were they just being nice? I let go of the breath I hadn't realized I had been holding in my lungs. Relief.

"Are you interested in anyone else right now?" Ella asked.

Oliver's face flashed through my mind. That crooked grin and goofy laugh. "God, no," I said. "I mean, maybe eventually, but it's just too soon, with Charlie and me in this state of limbo..."

"Limbo?" Ella frowned. "So, there's a chance you'll get back together or— wait, are you still together? I'm confused!"

I realized at that moment that I hadn't felt the complete permanence of my move into the house with Ella and Ivy. I had told myself that I was never going to be with Charlie ever again. It was the decision I had made. But I felt alone without him. *I was lonely.* I wanted to be thrilled. I liked that he kept coming after me, begging me to return to him. And when he did just that, I found it hard not to contemplate giving in to him.

But I had to admit I was kidding myself when I considered the possibility that anything would be different if I did give in to him. If we were to start over again...nothing would be different. He would still be the same Charlie, and I would still be the same me. And I wanted so much to change!

"There's really no chance we'll get back together," I responded, staring into the fire. "I just wish I could rid myself of this fantasy that I have, that if we get back together, I would suddenly have everything I want. I would suddenly be happy again."

"Bobbie, you don't need a guy to be happy, you know," Ella said.

"I get that," I said. And I did, intellectually. But for me being happy included being a girlfriend to a really great guy, a teammate.

Later in the night, after three glasses of Pinot Noir, my head was buzzing, and I felt emotionally drained. I said goodnight to the girls, who weren't ready to call it a night and made my way carefully down the stairs, and swan-dived onto my bed.

Charlie's face kept floating through my mind. I reminded myself of all the reasons I'd left him. The way he made me feel self-conscious about everything I believed in. The constant need to maintain perfection. The fact that I felt most alone when I was with him. Why couldn't I let go? What he thought about me, or anything else, really, was irrelevant. Was I blaming him for my unhappiness? Maybe my insecurities really had nothing to do with him at all. I shouldn't blame him. He's innocent. No, was not innocent. He cheated on me. You don't hurt the people you love. Wait, I forgave him and I should stick to that, based on principle. I need a vacation! No, I would still have to come back to this. I needed a change. I should quit my job and move across the country! No, I love Chicago and I would miss my friends and family too much. I needed therapy! But that's a sign of weakness. No, it's not, it's a sign of self-care. I needed to do something to take control of my life, or maybe I just needed to do less…Yeah…less is more.

My eyes grew heavy. I finally fell into a deep sleep and dreamed of Oliver. He was throwing pebbles into the lily pond at the zoo where we used to hang out together all the time. I was laughing with each great throw he made as more than ten ripples appeared as a result of each pebble tossed. I just kept laughing and thinking I had never seen anyone who was able to create so many ripples from a single throw.

Chapter Ten

"GOOD MORNING CHICAGOANS! What a great start to this beautiful fall day with 'Little Lion Man' by Mumford and Sons. Today's high will be 64 degrees and sunny, and tonight we'll have lows of 35..."

The morning radio woke me to a pounding headache. I rubbed my temples and realized I was still lying on top of my comforter. I slapped the radio, causing it to fall off my nightstand onto the floor. I left it. Lethargically walking to the bathroom, I heard Ella and Ivy awake already, primping in the bathroom together.

"She's a lightweight, that's for sure," I heard Ivy's voice. Were they talking about me? I stepped behind my door, trying to listen in.

"I think she's just a little insecure," Ella said. I couldn't believe they were talking about me. Were they talking about me?

"But I mean, who wouldn't be?" Ella continued,

"working in a modeling agency with all that competition, I don't know how she does it. On top of dating model boy!"

Yep. They're talking about me.

"I heard models are really bad in bed," Ivy said.

In my experience? *True.* I smiled sadly.

"Well, give her a chance. It's obvious she hasn't been single in a while and she's definitely a guy's girl. Try to be nice, would you?"

I felt sort of touched, that Ella would defend me.

"I'm nice, super nice, look at this face, nice written all over it," Ivy laughed. "I actually like her a lot."

I quietly shut my door, and then reopened loudly. "Good morning," I called.

"Morning!" they both shouted in unison. As I walked by on my way to the kitchen, I saw them looking at each other with some private signal. I think they knew I'd been listening. Great, I'm back in high school. I poured a cup of coffee. Suddenly, feeling suffocated in the apartment, I decided to go up to the roof to see what it looked like by early morning light.

The rush of cool air as I opened the door was refreshing. I breathed deep, walking over to the railing to look out over the city. There was nothing better than autumn in Chicago. My hot cup of my favorite vanilla roasted coffee in my hands felt comforting in contrast with the cool brisk air. I looked at the fire pit and the chairs, recalling events from the night before, sitting and talking with Ivy and Ella. On the ground were two empty bottles of wine and a pack of cigarettes. I smiled, picturing Ivy puffing away. They may not know the real me yet, I thought, but that wasn't their fault. Ella was right. I had some insecurities to deal with.

I tossed the wine bottles in the trash and noticed that tucked inside the pack of cigarettes was a lighter. *Oh, what the hell, I thought.* I hadn't smoked a cigarette since I was last in Italy. I lit one up and sucked the smoke deep into my lungs. On exhale I coughed so hard I thought I was going to pop a vessel. The idea of cigarettes was always more refreshing than they actually were. I crushed the cigarette out in the fire pit.

I heard the rusty door behind me slam. Startled, I turned back, grabbing the railing behind me.

"Meryl," I sighed.

"Jeez, someone's jumpy. Too much caffeine already?"

I grinned nervously. "Something like that."

"So, you like our little piece of heaven?"

I nodded. "Or 'cup of vino,' as Ivy calls it."

"I had the fire pit installed last year because

Barbara was complaining how chilly it was with the wind blowing, even in the summertime. But she rarely comes up here. I wish she would though." She smiled and rolling her eyes, added, "I just create the attractions. I can't make the audience come to the see the show!"

"Well, Ivy and Ella enjoy it," I said. "We got some use out of that fire pit last night."

Meryl saw the cigarette on the ground and looked at me, raising an eyebrow. "Seriously, are you okay? You seem..." She was trying to find the word, tip-toeing around my delicate feelings as usual. "nervous," she finished.

"No, really, I'm good. The girls and I had a great time up here last night. I drank too much and passed out on top of my bed sheets." I laughed at my pathetic drinking abilities.

"Well, look at you..." Meryl smirked.

I shook my head.

"I'm proud of you, Bobbie. You're going to be just fine," she said, and squeezed my arm. "I'm off to work. We're getting ready for the Chicago Arts and Artists Convention."

"Oh, I think Ivy was saying something about that last night. Her company is putting on the event, right?"

"Right. And I'll be there, supporting my writers. I was thinking of asking this guy Ryan Johnson as my date. I hate to go alone you know. What do you think?"

"Ryan? Ryan?"

"He's my assistant's brother. He's a tech entrepreneur, but he also is thinking about writing a book."

"Of course he is! Just like anyone who gets connected to you!" I laughed. "You should absolutely ask him."

"Okay, but if he turns me down, I'm going to ask *you* instead. You don't mind being second choice, do you?"

"Not in this case," I smiled.

"Oh, Barbara wanted me to tell you to stop by her place this morning before work."

"Okay," I agreed, wondering what Barbara had up her sleeve today.

On my way down, I knocked on Barbara's door. I heard barking, yelping, and Due's nails clattering towards the door. "Come in!" Barbara called. "Is that you, Bobbie?"

"Good morning, Barbara," I said. "Mmm. Smells good in here." The mingling smells of fresh baked bread and spices were tantalizing.

"Sit, sit. *Mangia, mangia.* I just made croissants!" She put two down in front of me, with a little dish of pumpkin butter.

"Wow, this looks incredible."

"I know you need to get off to work, but I just wanted to give you something."

"Something else?"

"Man does not live by bread alone—and neither does woman!" She handed me a small leather-bound book. On top of it was a post-it note reading *obscuris vera involvens.*

"This helped me in my darkest of times. Happy reading, dolly!" She laid a big kiss on my cheek.

Chapter Eleven

During my lunch break, I sat down at my desk and opened the book Barbara had given me. The title page read *Obscuris Vera Involvens.* "In darkness lies truth." I knew some Latin from my mother forcing it down my throat growing up, as well as knowing Italian, Portuguese, and French. *Life is nothing without knowledge of romance, Roberta.* I could still hear her voice ringing in my head. But she was always more interested in the romance *languages* than what actually went on between lovers.

The first page was handwritten in perfect calligraphy: *According to Greek mythology, humans were originally created with four arms, four legs, and a head with two faces. Fearing their power, Zeus split them into two separate parts, condemning them to spend their lives in search of their other halves.*

"Slacking, darling?"

I looked up to see the striking face of Wolfgang

Lutz, my boss. I closed the book and gave him my full attention. "Just taking a small lunch break," I said. "Nice of you to drop by."

"Bobbie," he said, "I want you to go try on that red Reem Acra dress in the studio."

I looked at him stupidly. Did he get hit on the head and confuse me with one of the models or something?

"Long sleeves? Lace?" He tapped his foot impatiently.

"Yes, I know the one..."

"If it fits, it's yours." He threw a large, fat envelope down on my desk. "And could you be a dream and look these papers over for me? Tell me if those horrid people have *any* sort of a leg to stand on."

"What is this?" I slid the papers out of the envelope, fanned them out a little. "But these are all concerning Jack's clients, not mine."

"I realize that, but I want you to look over the paperwork and tell me what you think. Jack's been super busy, and—" he cast a lingering glance over my neat desk and my book, as if to imply that I wasn't busy, or at least not busy enough, "—and you have such a head for contracts. I always know I can count on you."

The flattery found its mark. Wolfe knew what

energized me, and he played right to it. After all, that was his genius, and why he ran one of the top modeling agencies in the world.

"Okay. So you want me to look over the papers and...give you a report?"

"Yes! A *report*. Perfect."

"By when? When do you need it?"

"Well, it won't do me any good if it's not done immediately," he said. "And Bobbie...don't tell Jack, or anyone else, that I asked you to do this."

I bit my lower lip and frowned. "But if—"

"Bobbie," he said, interrupting me. "Go try on that dress. Now." He actually snapped his fingers at me.

I made my way down the cold white hallway towards the studio, opening the heavy steel door. There, on a rack with a couple of other pieces, hung a beautiful lace dress in my own trademark red. I wanted to touch it, and yet I was afraid to taint it somehow. Forgetting for a moment my wariness about this whole deal of Wolfe's, I carefully took the dress off the hanger and walked towards the dressing room.

I stopped in my tracks when I heard crying from the bathroom lounge. I opened the door and saw Lilly sitting on the love seat with her hands over her face, tissues scattered everywhere as tears streamed down her cheeks.

"Lilly, are you okay?" I'd never seen her like this. She was always so perky, like a golden retriever.

She collected herself quickly, sitting up straight, attempting to fix her crazed hair.

"Peachy!" She forced a smile. Her mascara formed dark rings under her eyes.

"What's going on?" I asked, concerned, sitting down beside her.

"I'm okay." She leaned over and hugged me. Even in grief she invaded my personal space. *Watch the dress!*

"My boyfriend cheated on me!" she sobbed.

I patted her back, attempting to console her. For a moment it occurred to me to tell her we were in the same boat, but something held me back. I wanted to think of myself as somehow different than Lilly. *She's* pathetic, I thought. Me, I'm—what? Also pathetic. "Lilly, how old are you?"

"Nineteen," she whimpered.

"That's right, you're nineteen. By the time I was your age, I had blown through dozens of boys, and may I emphasize *boys*, not men."

"Of course you did. You're beautiful, and I know, I'm ugly and awkward." She sobbed harder.

"Stop feeling sorry for yourself. You're not ugly or

awkward. You are beautiful, creative, and one of the most original girls I've ever known."

"Really?" She looked at me hopefully.

"Guys your age are young, immature, and have absolutely no idea who they are yet. It doesn't help that women are surpassing them in everything. I think there's even a study that says our brains are more developed than theirs at that age. A boy who cheats is a boy who is lost and doesn't know what he wants. Try to understand, it's not about you. You don't need a guy to make you feel special. That's *your* job."

I felt guilty, giving her advice that I couldn't follow myself. Then again, talking to a nineteen-year-old did put things in perspective. I had lived more life, dated more men, traveled more places. All that experience had to count towards something, right?

"Yeah, you're absolutely right," she said, sucking up her snot. "But it just hurts so bad." She threw her head onto my shoulder, wiping her tears away. "And I just feel like, if only I was more…"

"If you were more…what? Beautiful? Talented? Witty?" She certainly couldn't hope to be any thinner, I thought.

"Yes, all those things. And some other stuff too."

"Okay, so what if you were all that. Then what?"

"He'd be knocking at my door, wanting me back, and I could feel whole again." She started sobbing even louder. *Oh the drama...*

Back to square one. A strange part of me wanted to hunt down the jerk who broke this innocent bird-like girl's heart. Seeing Lilly set back by life's common tragedy was heart-wrenching. She had done nothing to deserve this pain. But I guess a few bumps and bruises along the journey toward the pursuit of love only makes you smarter in the long run. Why should Lilly be deprived of such a valuable experience?

"Lilly, you can choose to wallow in self-pity or you can ditch that insecure little boy who needs to have more than one girl holding him up because he can't support himself on his own. I think you should go home, get a bottle of wine or some ice cream, and be with your friends."

"Okay," she said compliantly. She fell into my arms with a big, awkwardly warm hug.

"Thank you," she whispered. "Only, I try not to overindulge in alcohol or food."

"Fine," I said with a laugh. "You're ahead of the game with that one! I think friends are the key component, anyway."

Her face crumpled up again. "But he was my *very*

best friend!" she wailed.

Lilly finally calmed down enough to go back to work. After picking up the wet tissues and washing my hands, I kicked off my shoes, undressed and slipped into the red lace dress. As I pulled the zipper up and buttoned the three small buttons, I turned to face the mirror, and...I smiled...broadly. I held my hair up, then let it down, held it up, and let it down. Half up, half down, curled...*yes*. I slipped on the heels I wore to the office, even though they didn't match the dress. My legs looked pretty good, I thought. *Dance classes with Ella must be paying off.*

I walked into the empty studio to look at myself in the larger mirrors, my phone buzzed.

"Hey Meryl."

"So, I need a favor! Will you please, *please* come to the Arts Convention with me on Saturday?"

"I thought you had a date?"

"My date, well...it's not happening."

"Ah, I'm sorry."

"It's okay. I'll tell you about it later. So, can you go?"

"Let's get this straight," I said. "You want me to get all glammed up to see Chicago's hottest artists with my best friend? I can think of nothing worse. But if you insist, I will go. You owe me one."

"I love you. You know Ivy's PR firm is putting on the event, so she'll be there too. Maybe she can sneak Ella in. Girls' night! Oh, stupid question, but do you have a dress?"

"Yes," I said, checking myself in the big studio mirrors. "I believe I *do*."

"Great. I don't, so I'm going shopping tomorrow after work. You wanna meet me? Help me find something amazing?"

"Shopping? It's what I do best."

Behind me the studio door swung open, startling me. I lost my balance. Oliver quickly stepped up and steadied me.

"Whoa, sorry. I didn't know anyone was in here!" he said. His hands were firm, and they lingered on my arms just a moment longer than necessary.

"Meryl, I'll call you back, okay? Bye." I hung up. "Hey, Olly!"

"Sorry to startle you."

"Don't be, really."

"What are you doing?"

I stood tall and presented my dress. "Wolfe gave it to me."

"Wolfe gave it to you?" he asked incredulously.

"Yep. It was a bribe."

"A bribe? For what?"

"Can't tell you. It's secret legal business. So, do you like it?"

"Yeah, looks great," he said expressionlessly. Not exactly the response I was looking for. "Well, I was just looking for Lilly," he said. "I thought I saw her come in here."

"Looking for Lilly, huh?" I said. "Oh, that's right, she kind of likes you, doesn't she?"

"She's got some prints of mine, I hope. Have you seen her?"

"I have. But I don't know where she went."

"Well—" He hesitated, looked me up and down. "Where's my camera when I need it?" he murmured staring at me. "I guess...I'll see you later, Bobbie." He turned to go.

"Wait, Olly," I stopped him. "Before you go, will you unzip my dress for me?" I turned around.

"Sure," he said hesitantly. I heard him blow into his hands and rub them together. "Sorry, my hands are—"

"You're fine," I said. He stepped in closer. I felt his finger on the top of my spine, fingers fumbling with the buttons, his hands not cold at all. When the three little top buttons were undone, he slowly unzipped the dress.

"There, yup—uh—anything else?"

Was he nervous? How incredibly adorable, I thought, laughing inside. "No, that's all," I said. "Thank you." In the mirror I could see him hurrying towards the door with his hands shoved into his pockets. "Bye..."

"I'll see ya, Bobbie," he called with a wave, as something fell from his pocket—a pen. But he was already gone.

I slipped off the dress, hung it back on the rack, and got dressed in my work clothes. On my way out of the studio I picked up Oliver's pen, which was one of those personalized ones. I did a double take. The white on black cursive script read: *Oliver Prince Gallery of Arts and Design.*

But Oliver doesn't have a gallery, I thought. I mean, he'd often talked about putting something together, but I didn't think he'd actually got that far on it...Or had I been too self-absorbed to notice?

I stuck the pen behind my ear and hustled to my office, breezing past the secretaries, hoping they wouldn't try to stop me in hopes of delegating their duties. It was bad enough that my boss did that to me all the time.

I had made it through the gauntlet, and was just

about to shut my door.

"Oh, Roberta—"

"You rang?" I peeked my head out of my office.

"You're behind on setting the Brazilians for the Centennial shoot..." British Alice smacked her gum.

Ah yes. The Centennial. The Centennial had been all the rave at Fordham Agency for at least the past month or more. To celebrate the 100th anniversary of Fordham Agency, we were pulling in models from all over the world for a big photo shoot before the holidays. Chicago was about turn into a model mecca. The stress in the office was magnified because we had only a short window in which to conduct the shoots. LA's Fashion Week was the day after our last day of shooting, meaning all of our models needed to be there. Wolfe was running about the office like a madman.

"I'm on it!" I said to Alice, shutting my office door. I quickly sat down at my desk and typed into the Google search bar: *Oliver Prince Gallery of Arts and Design.*

The link for the site popped up, followed by links for Facebook, Twitter, and LinkedIn. I clicked on his site. Up came a sleek, simple yet stunning homepage of black and white photography, with Oliver's name in classy cursive font at the top. *What? How did I not know about this?* He had never mentioned it. How oblivious was I to the fact that Oliver had been quietly building his empire while working here? I knew he did independent shoots, but there was always the risk of a conflict of interest contract being breached here at Fordham. Maybe that's why he'd been so low-key about it.

I clicked the "About" page and up came Oliver's photo. He was looking down, laughing, and I knew that smile so well. It was perfectly sincere. It made *me* smile, knowing the picture was a candid shot. Though he was at home behind the lens, he was terribly bashful in front of it. Next to his picture there was a short bio and a list of services offered: *Photography, Design, Graphic Arts, Digital Marketing, Branding.* Following that was an impressive array of credentials, recommendations, and endorsements; top designer brands Oliver had worked for, countries he'd worked in. The site was available in Italian, Portuguese, French, Spanish, Chinese, and a few other flags I didn't recognize. What was he *up* to?

At the bottom of the page was an address, which I copied and pasted it into Google Maps. I was creeping hard. A warehouse in Wicker Park, with a link to "Look Inside." I clicked, zoomed in. It was a gallery, clean and sleek. Glass tables, Apple computers, hanging bulb lights; it looked fabulous. I couldn't believe this. I wanted to run and find Oliver to hound him with questions. Then again, maybe I'd just wait and see how long it took him to tell me himself.

I finished my work as quickly as I could, scheduling models here, booking flights to Chicago O'Hare from Belo Horizonte, Sao Paolo, Rio, and Bahia in time for the Centennial shoot. Then I spent several hours working on the "secret" project Wolfe had given me. I felt pretty proud of myself, having zeroed in on a number of issues that might conceivably cause him problems, along with some possible solutions. I was just about ready to make a quick exit, when my phone buzzed and my stomach dropped. *Charlie.* He hadn't called in days, and I was beginning to get used to it. I silenced the phone, my nerves tingled through every inch of my body. But I was just too curious. I gave in.

"Hello?"

"Ignoring me still?"

"I've been busy, Charlie."

"I've been thinking about you a lot. And about *us.* What are you doing Saturday night?"

"I have plans, actually," I stated boldly.

"I have a table at the Chicago Arts Convention. Go

with me?"

No, no, no, this city is not big enough for the two of us. Why did he always have to come tearing into my world?

"Funny you should mention it. I'm already going with someone." I left out that it was Meryl. I wanted him to be jealous. I wanted him to know he wasn't my life—not anymore. "In fact, my roommate's PR firm is putting on the event."

"Then I'll see you there," he said, and hung up.

I pranced into Wolfe's office the next morning, very pleased with myself. I had stayed up half the night getting my special report organized for him. I had rewritten it several times, trying to put it in language that Wolfe would understand. It wasn't that he was stupid, but he had a very short attention span.

He looked up at me without smiling when his secretary showed me in.

"Bobbie," he said. "I'm right in the middle of something. I hope whatever you're bothering me about is important."

I waited for Alma to shut the door. "I brought you the report," I said.

He looked at me blankly.

"Regarding the papers you asked me to look at?"

I prompted.

"Oh, yes, did you bring back that envelope I gave you?"

"Yes, it's in here with my report." I handed him the folder. "I read over all the papers, and I made detailed notes on—"

"So, this is everything I gave you, right?" Without even opening the folder, he pulled out the envelope and handed me back the report. The report I had spent hours compiling. "I don't need that," he said. "I talked to our attorneys, and they're going to take care of everything. So, did you get those flights set up for the models?"

The blood rushed my head and pounded in my face. I wanted to scream. *Was he kidding?* Wolfe could pull some real crap. But I was shocked by this.

"Bobbie?" he asked impatiently. "Did you take care of the flights, or not?"

"Yes," I replied sharply. "Not to worry. It's all handled."

"All right. So—anything else? No? You know what to do then?"

"Yes," I said slowly. "Yes, I know exactly what to do."

Chapter Twelve

I smoothed my dress as it hung from my closet door, caressing the red lace embroidery from neckline to knee. I looked into my mirror as I stood in my bra and underwear. I looked slender and strong. As I traced a line with my finger along my collarbones, over my ribs, down to my belly, I took two steps closer to the mirror to look myself in the eye. I looked good, but I was missing something, I thought, something that I not only wanted but that I needed. Charlie? He could still agitate me, sure. But I was getting over him. He haunted me less and less these days. I smoothed my hair, noticing its lushness. I touched my lips, noticing their plump kissability. I brushed my lashes, noticing their long fluttering beauty. I had to admit—I was beautiful tonight.

"Eye lash curler?" I heard the voices from Ella and Ivy's bathroom.

I came in to visit, wearing my silk robe. The two

of them stood inches away from the mirror, side by side, as usual.

"Hair spray?" Ella asked.

"Right next to you," Ivy responded, curling her lashes.

"Got it."

"My God," I said to Ivy, "Your lashes are so long. How do you get them to look like that?"

"Well, years of practice, I guess, and my lashes are naturally long, so that helps," she added modestly.

All of a sudden there was a huge thud from the ceiling. Then another, and another. Ella and Ivy looked at each other. "It's Barbara," said Ivy. "That's her signal!" We all ran up the stairs in our robes and bare feet.

"Dollies, Meryl told me you're all going to a ball tonight."

"We are!"

"No dates?" she asked.

We shook our heads.

"Well good, more fun that way. Where is Meryl?"

"She's meeting us there."

"Well, dollies, I called you up here because I figured that since the temperature has dropped to record lows for October, you'd be needing coats. Follow me!" She led us into her opulent bedroom, towards the closet of folding mirrors. When she flung open the doors, we gasped. The entire closet was filled with rows of fur coats and vintage boxes filled with designer hats, scarves, and gloves.

"Take your pick," she said, with a flourish. "I truly would not buy a fur today, but I can't bear to get rid of the ones I have."

The closet smelled of rich leather and expensive perfume. Thrilled, we sifted through the coats and opened boxes. Barbara reached for a chocolate colored mink, handing it to me with a wink. It was beyond perfection. I slipped into it, the silk lining delicate against my sensitive skin. I hugged myself in utter bliss, as if I were engulfed in creamy dark chocolate.

Ivy and Ella tried on white, brown, and black furs, giggling and twirling in the mirrors. Finally, we each stood in our coats, looking for Barbara's approval. It was like playing dress-up as kid, only this was real.

"Are these the ones you like?" she asked. "You've each got your favorite?"

"Yes!" the three of us said in unison.

"Then keep them," she said. "They're yours."

"No, Barbara," Ella said.

"We couldn't," I added.

"I'm not getting any younger, dollies, and I believe it's quite apparent that I have more coats than a department store, certainly more than I need. Please, my gift to my babies."

"Well, I have to say, this does look fabulous on me," Ivy said, gazing at herself in the mirror. We all laughed. We felt like movie stars.

I hung my new mink near my dress and went into my bathroom to finish getting ready.

"Bobbie!" I heard my name being called. Ivy poked her head around the corner. "Why don't you come get ready with us in our bathroom?"

She disappeared as quickly as she had come. I looked at myself in my little mirror, a big smile spreading across my face.

I gathered up all my hair stuff and my makeup bag and carried it into their bathroom, gingerly making room on the already overcrowded countertop.

"Ooh," said Ivy. "Can I try this eye shadow? Mind sharing?"

I shook my head. "I don't mind."

"Here," she said. "This red lipstick will go great with your dress."

"Do you think I could borrow that big curling iron?" Ella asked me. "I've been meaning to get one like this…"

That was the moment I felt pure female acceptance. I wanted to savor it like a fine wine. Ella taught me how to make my eyelashes look like hers, and I fixed her hair into calm curls. I borrowed Ivy's bold red lipstick, and Ivy browsed my perfume collection.

"My God," she said. "I'm in awe of the sheer number of bottles you have. But you always wear Coco Chanel!"

"I just love all the different bottles," I said happy to share my obsession. "I think they're so beautiful. Every girl has her favorite accessory. Perfume's mine."

I was the last one finished. I'd sprayed the last curl, perfected my mascara, slipped on my heels and jewelry, spritzed my Coco Chanel, and walked into the dining room for approval. Ivy waited in her gorgeous navy gown with a bottle of something in her hand.

"Shots?" I laughed.

Ella rolled her eyes. "Are you surprised?"

"What? You expect me to go *sober* to this thing? Awkward!" Ivy handed me a glass.

"What is it?"

"Goldschlager."

"Good God. Someone's going big tonight!" Ella said.

There was no denying—Ivy liked to party.

"Well, I got it for free!" she said with a wink. "Along

with two other bottles. The perks of working in PR! They're a sponsor at the event tonight. And with the sponsor line-up for this evening, ladies, you can expect gold toilets and the bathroom attendant to wipe your ass for you!"

"Ivy!" Ella shouted, attempting to tame her as usual.

"Cheers!" I raised my glass.

"—to looking hot!" Ella shouted.

"And pooping in a golden pot!" Ivy swigged.

"Don't—don't make me laugh so hard," I managed to say between fits of giggles. "I don't want to have to start over with the make-up." But the laughter was uncontrollable. Watching Ivy dance like a demented leprechaun was more than I could take. Our merriment was threatening to ruin our carefully crafted costumes, but we were having too much fun to care. It suddenly occurred to me that for the first time since I moved in, I had allowed myself to completely let go and be myself with my girls. I had forgotten what it was like to feel like an outsider.

Chapter Thirteen

I felt the cold air on my legs as we climbed out of the cab. As we walked in, I spotted Meryl standing at the top of the stairs. After checking our coats in the lobby, the four of us made our grand entrance. The music bumped like "Planet Lounge Radio" on my Pandora list. I could feel my hips wanting to move with the beat.

Three women smelling of gin and tonic stared at the four of us as we strode down the hall. "Is that—what's her name?" one of them asked in a stage whisper.

"Who?" said her friend.

"You know. *What's her name?*"

When we'd walked out of earshot, I said in a low voice, "You know it was me they were talking about, right? I'm told I look just like *what's her name.*"

"No, no, it was me," Ella said. "I'm a dead ringer for *what's her name.*"

"You're both wrong," said Ivy. "Everyone knows I'm the spittin' image of—"

"What's her name!" The three of us shouted. Heads turned. Meryl looked at us with concern.

"Sorry, Meryl," I giggled. "We've had Goldschlager."

Just before we made it to the ballroom, we had to walk the red carpet. Broadcast reporters, radio personalities, photographers, and two women with iPads stood at the photo booth near the entrance.

"Name?" asked a skinny girl with a clipboard.

"Roberta Bertucci," I replied, resisting the urge to say, *"What's her name."*

"Miss Bertucci, who are you wearing tonight?" she asked.

Proudly, I said: "Red Reem by Acra."

"Fabulous," she purred. Snap! Pop! Flash! I continued into the ballroom alone as the girls got their photos taken. The room was jaw-dropping gorgeous with rows of hanging chandeliers and swags of red velvet draped over enormous windows. I looked up to see a Renaissance-style painted ceiling that made me feel as if I were back in a Roman church: hand-painted cherubs, naked men and women surrounded by fruits and clouds. A Spanish guitarist stood playing beside a grand piano, and servers in black and white circled the party with champagne and crab cakes. Ivy's PR firm really knew how to throw a fabulous event. The room smelled of cologne, red wine, and the brisk fall air blowing in from the street. My heels clacked on the cold marble flooring, as a waiter handed me a glass of champagne.

I scanned the room to see if I recognized anyone.

FLASH! POP! I turned as I sipped to see top model Alessandra Valentino—blonde, beautiful, and legs for days—emerge from the crowd of paparazzi near the entrance of the gala. Everyone was bending over backwards to take her picture as she entered the room. Behind her, with his hand resting lightly on the small of her back was—*Charlie!*

Two women standing near me were talking. "You see that?" one of them said, looking at Charlie and Alessandra Valentino walking in together. "I heard this is their public debut together."

"Oh, come now. Everyone knows she's been sneaking around with some mystery man for months, now."

"Really, everyone?"

"Well, her husband just found out. But everyone else!"

I swallowed a gulp of champagne, and it almost

came out of my nose as I began to choke. My eyes welled from the bubbles coming out of my nose.

"Jesus, Bobbie, are you okay?" Meryl asked, patting my back, handing me a napkin. She looked over and saw Charlie. "Oh God, okay, bathroom, bathroom..." She tried to guide me away.

"No, no, honestly, it's no big deal," I said, shrugging her hand off of my shoulder. "I'm fine."

"Are you sure?" she gazed at me with concern.

"Positive," I stated, wiping my nose of any champagne that was still possibly dripping out.

Charlie and Alessandra? Could it be true? I downed the rest of my glass and waved the server over for another. Watching Charlie, so proud of his trophy, smiling at cameras, and flipping his hair, I started laughing. His shallowness was so blindingly obnoxious. Ivy, Ella, and Meryl looked at me, worried, and then looked at each other.

"Guys, honestly. I'm fine. I promise you. It's downright amusing to me. Alessandra! This will be really good for his career...and ego. That only makes me look better." I looked at Charlie and Alessandra with dollar signs in my eyes.

"All right then," Meryl said. "Let's celebrate! Cheers." She raised her glass. "To what's good for your career!"

"Cheers," I said. "To the girls of 721 Dearborn, the best friends a girl could have!" And I meant it. They had been there for me through all of this. I felt lucky to have them in my life.

We made our way toward the gallery of fine art and photography where Meryl introduced me to a few of her colleagues and columnists who worked for *Chicago Magazine*, the *Chicago Tribune* and the *Sun Times*. I smiled, shook hands, smiled, shook hands; but in the back of my head, I marveled at the pure numbness I felt for Charlie. When I saw him walk in with Alessandra, he had suddenly struck me as a manikin, perfectly plastic, with zero substance. The air in the room suddenly felt freer. I found myself able to breathe, as if I'd been holding my breath for days.

I felt a tap on my back. "Who's the hottie snapping pictures of you, Bobbie?" Ivy asked, playing with the olive in her empty martini glass.

"What?" I turned around to scan the room and to see who she was talking about. Oliver. My stomach lurched oddly as my gaze met his. He looked tall and trim in his black tie. His eyes had a power over me. I couldn't look away. He waved. I smiled. "That's Oliver. You met him once, remember? Maybe you were too drunk to remember. Oliver is an awesome photographer. We've been friends forever."

"Uh, huh," Ivy said, looking at me, then back to Oliver and back at me.

"He's just a friend," I repeated, and nudged her.

"Well, your friend is coming over here."

As I watched Oliver gliding toward us through the crowd, it was like someone turned up the heat and sucked all the air out of the room. I fidgeted and fixed my hair, feeling suddenly shy and uneasy. *Put your hand down, quit playing with your hair. What is wrong with you?*

Before I could utter a hello, he leaned in and kissed me on the cheek, taking my hand and twirling me around. He stepped back and scanned me from head to toe. In a pompous English accent he said, "My, oh my, Miss Bobbie Bertucci, don't you look ravishing this evening.

I elbowed him playfully. "Shut up."

He looked hurt. "What? You *do* look ravishing."

"You're so full of it. Oliver, you remember Ivy, my roommate."

"Hey," he said. "Nice to see you again."

They shook hands. Ivy leaned in and whispered something in his ear that made him laugh. He looked at me with an enigmatic smile as Ivy walked away.

"Hey," I called after her. "Where you going?"

"Bar," she called over her shoulder. "Must get drink."

Olly held out his arm for me. "Shall we?"

"We shall," I said.

We walked across the crowded room together, arm in arm, following Ivy to the bar.

Oliver was leaning up against the bar, talking to the bartender, when a blonde woman in a long black dress came up behind him, touching his arm to get his attention. Her eye makeup was dark and black, her lips golden. "Mr. Prince," she said, "your work, it's just *phenomenal*. I heard you're opening up shop." She held her white wine out to the side as her body swayed towards him.

"You heard right," he said.

I felt jealous. It was a professional jealousy, I told myself. Besides, we were friends, right? Good friends. Why had he not mentioned this to me? I had thought maybe it was a private project he was keeping secret until it was time to unveil, but no. This total stranger was all dialed in. And others too, judging by the comments people were making and the congratulations he was receiving. Everyone seemed to

Shy Town Girls

know about it. Everyone. Except me.

"I'd like to stop by your studio sometime when you're free," the blonde said, seduction dripping from her voice. She was disgustingly forward, I thought.

"Yeah, sure," Oliver said as he brushed back his hair. He seemed a little nervous with the attention on him. I wished she'd leave. No doubt she wished *I* would leave, too, but I stood my ground at Olly's side. She peered at me with her frost blue eyes and allowed a half smile, girl code for *competition, bitch.*

"I want to introduce you to some people," she said. "Don't go away."

"Sorry about that," Oliver said out of the side of his mouth when she turned away.

"For what?"

"I think you should dance with me," he answered. He reached out to take my hand, but the moment was ruined by the return of the skanky blonde, who deliberately pushed herself between us. She dragged over her friends, a bunch of artsy wine and cheese connoisseurs, who probably took frequent vacations to Aspen and Naples in the winter months.

"How are you? Pleasure to meet you," Oliver said, shaking hands. The blonde girl leaned into Oliver and stroked his arm, then his back, as she introduced him, giggling for no apparent reason.

I decided to let Olly network. I slipped away and surveyed the room, looking for my friends. None of the girls were in sight so I made my way to the art exhibit. Moments later I found myself lost in a black and white photo of a young woman wearing nothing but a man's dress coat, sitting on the edge of a brick apartment building overlooking the city, smoking a cigarette. It was very Tim Burton-esque, with the dark shadows, dark make-up, and the backdrop of Chicago looking strangely distorted. The woman looked sad, sucking down her cigarette, but maybe that wasn't the case at all. Maybe she was at peace in this great city she loved, sitting on top of the world just before dawn, watching over Chicago while the rest of world was asleep, wrapped in her lover's jacket that smelled of cologne and scotch.

I loved it.

"Mmm..." I heard the low throaty animal growl from behind me as two strong hands grabbed hold of my hips and a large male body pressed up to mine. Shocked and startled, I turned to see Charlie's bold eyes looking deep into mine.

"Leave with me," he said.

"Whoa," I responded, pushing his hands off of my

hips, stepping back. "Charlie!"

"Still playing hard to get, huh?"

"I'm not playing with you, Charlie. And I'm not sure what else I can do to convince you of that. It's *over* between us." I marveled at the calm strength in my own voice. "It's over."

"C'mon Bobbie. Did you not see who I came with tonight? *Leave with me.*"

"I'm not going anywhere with you, Charlie. We're done."

"Leave with me now, Roberta—*you know you want to.* And I'm warning you, I'm not going to ask you again."

"Excuse me, but is that a promise—or a threat, Charlie?"

"You can take it as a warning."

"You are disgusting." I turned away, but he grabbed my arm and made me face him.

"Would you just let go and take a risk?" he said, his voice pleading now. "You're so calculated."

"Is he bothering you, Bobbie?"

Charlie and I had been so focused on one another, like two alley cats exchanging insults. I looked over my shoulder to see Oliver eyeing us. He gave me a *is everything okay* look and I nodded. He scrunched his eyebrows.

Charlie loosened his grip on my arm and dropped his hand, looking at Oliver with a disdainful expression.

Oliver broke away from the crowd that surrounded him and began to walk over fire in his eyes. I gave him a stern look and a little wave. Reluctantly, he backed off. Giving me one last, pointed look, Olly wandered away.

"Oh my God," Charlie said incredulously. "So *that's* what's going on? You're screwing the photographer."

"What?"

"You've been hanging out with that sap!" He threw his head back and laughed hysterically.

"Oliver is my best friend," I said coolly. "We've known each other since we were basically kids."

"He's a square, always has been. He's not your *friend*, Bobbie. You look to guys like Oliver to feed your ego. To boost your pathetic confidence. That's all."

"Excuse me? Oliver's a real friend, a genuine person. Something you know nothing about," I said.

"Every guy's nice until they get in your pants, Bobbie. That's how it goes."

"No, that's just how you are."

"I don't know where you come off thinking I should be kissing your ass 24/7. I'm not that guy, Bobbie."

"No," I said, "you're not *that* guy—or any other I'd want to be with for that matter."

"My date thinks otherwise, don't you think?" He looked around for Alessandra, who had been swallowed up by a sea of admirers.

"Great," I said. "I'm happy for you—you've replaced me. I feel bad for the next girl that has to put up with your shit. I wish you both well. Now, if you'll excuse me—"

"You underestimate me, Bobbie," he said. "And you underestimate yourself. I want you, and you need me. Make your choice now, because at the end of the night it's going to be either him or me. And you know who you want. And it isn't that second-rate hack photographer."

I felt a lump rise in my throat and my face turn white-hot. He was pathetic, empty, and ugly. I wanted to scream at him for insulting not only Oliver but me, for the pain he caused me, for all the lies I bought and for wasting my time, but instead I went with my second impulse. SLAP! I laid all five fingers across Charlie's million-dollar face. "Don't you ever insult me or him. Are we clear?" I said in a cold voice. I heard gasps, and people were staring as I made my way to the exit. I didn't look back.

I was standing at the coat check waiting for my fur when I heard Meryl's voice calling. "Whoa, whoa, whoa. What do you think you're doing?"

"Leaving."

"Are you serious, Bobbie? Why?"

"If I stay, I'll murder Charlie."

"What did he do? Actually no, I don't want to know because I'll want to murder him too. Bobbie, please stay. Don't let him ruin your night—your life—like he's done since day one! This is your time. Don't let him be in charge of it."

She was right. It was stupid to let him get to me as usual, allowing him to ruin the night. I realized I hadn't even asked her what had happened with to her date. I felt a sudden rush of guilt.

"You're right, Meryl," I said. We walked back to the ballroom together, and I felt defiant. Charlie was all over his new model girlfriend. Oliver was nowhere to be found.

"Meryl, can you excuse me for a few minutes?" I asked.

She gave me a look.

"I just want to get some air. I'm not going anywhere, I promise." My face still hot.

"Okay." She winked.

I stepped out onto the balcony. The only other people on the balcony were two smokers near the railing with their orange tips glowing in the dark. I looked out at the panorama of the city. It was stunning; impeccable. I sighed, attempting to fill my lungs with the fresh night air. I stared into the darkness above the city lights to clear my head. I wanted to fly, to escape. I wanted things to be simple. I wanted freedom. I closed my eyes.

"Don't jump," said a voice. I turned around to see Oliver standing with his head down, looking at me from under his brow, hands in pockets.

"Wasn't gonna," I said. His suit fit him well, or he fit the suit, I wasn't sure which it was—but he looked sharp.

"You look beautiful Bobbie," he said, coming to stand beside me, leaning against the railing. His tone was different now, no longer the silly British accent he'd used before when he'd complimented me.

"Thanks," I blushed. "And thanks for—in there— I'm sorry." I stuttered. He wanted to defend me against Charlie, but I had to do it myself. He always knew when I needed him, always leading me to find some light in the dark.

"What's going on, you?" he asked.

"Just getting some air."

"I don't mean right now, but what's going on with your life...*you* know. With him."

"Charlie and I are...I don't know." I felt embarrassed, too shy to go into detail.

"Just let go," he blurted.

"What?" He had sounded like Charlie there for a moment.

"Look Bobbie, you're a gorgeous girl, and equally as weird and complicated."

"Well, you know me better than anyone, don't you?"

"That's 'cause I've seen you through all your phases. Like your rock star phase when you only listened to angry lesbian girl bands. And your hippie phase when you joined Greenpeace and you made me call the Argentinean Embassy. I know that you like to lock yourself in your room and listen to emo music, and I know how you eat tomatoes even though you hate them because you think they're good for your heart. This and that, Charlie, it's a phase."

"Hey, I still like those angry girl bands," I laughed at the memory.

"What I'm saying is, you have a history, we have a history. So, I think I'm entitled to point out that you could do a lot better. You don't need that guy in your life, bringing you down to bring himself up."

The smokers had gone inside. In the silence the wind whistled over the hum of voices from inside.

I exhaled. "I know," I said giving in.

"You do?" he asked, looking at me with his head cocked sideways. I nodded in assurance that I understood him, and he was right. He ran his fingers through his hair and itched his nose. "Well, all right, then. By the way, your roommates are great. Ivy keeps hitting on me."

"When she's drunk she hits on everyone. Don't get too excited."

"Don't tell me that. I thought she really liked me. And you know I need all the ego boost I can get," he grinned.

"Olly?"

"Yeah?" Crossing his arms again.

"Why didn't you tell me that you're opening a gallery?"

"I did," he shrugged. "Didn't I?"

"I mean, you talked about it, but...I feel like I was the last to know. I guess I thought we were closer than that. When I saw your web site..."

"Hey, it's really no big deal. I don't know. I guess...I

didn't know if I was going to be successful or not when I decided to do my own thing. I didn't want to disappoint you or myself really."

"Disappoint? You're crazy. I just wish you had told me sooner. I wished I didn't have to find out through the grapevine. I would've wanted to help you."

"I've still got a long way to go, Bobbie, but luckily I have a few loyal clients to keep me afloat while I get my feet on the ground. Sorry. I know how you hate it when I mix my metaphors."

"When do you leave?"

"Leave Fordham?"

"Yeah."

"I'm done. Haven't you noticed I haven't been around as much?" He laughed, and I think he felt somewhat offended.

"I did notice," I said. "But I thought you were out on assignment. So, you left before the Centennial! Wolfie must have had a fit."

"I told him I'd help him out if he needed me. He didn't seem to think he'd need me."

"And you don't need—Fordham." I was about to say, "we."

"I really have no emotional ties to that place, Bobbie. It wasn't hard. I'm really not about what that place is all about."

"I know. You're too good for it." I affirmed.

"There's plenty more talented photographers than me Bobbie," he informed.

"I'm not talking about just your photography." He was too good of a person for the industry. His photos could change the world.

My heart sank to the depths of my stomach as I pictured myself without Olly in that white, hospital-like, florescent lit building filled with insatiable human beings starving for approval.

"I'm sorry, Olly. My head's been up my ass. I'm gonna miss that over-roasted coffee."

"You know, if you play your cards right, you might not have to go without. I'd like you to come by and see the new studio. I can make you coffee there."

"I'd like that."

"Good," he smiled.

I grinned, blushing. We leaned toward each other and almost bumped foreheads. "Oops," I said, "Sorry."

"Shall we?" he cocked his arm, gesturing me to link. I ignored his arm and threw my arms around him, hugging him, holding him close. I felt his heart racing against my chest. His hands cold on my back.

As I drew away, he didn't let go of me. His arms

were around me. I felt his body warm and firm against mine. I looked up at him and saw that expression in his eyes—the soulful one that always got me questioning. *What's going on behind that cheerful, yet calm personality of his?* He leaned in closer, still staring into my eyes. I was suddenly seized with panic. I pulled out of his embrace. Shivering at the sudden loss of his warmth, I wrapped my arms around myself and forced a smile. He cleared his throat.

"Look at you freezing in this little dress. Next time wear a turtleneck would you? And sweatpants. And no make-up. And yeah, I'm not okay with all these hounds checking you out all night," he murmured, slipping his jacket off and draping it over my shoulders. It smelled good—like him. "We'd better get you inside. Dance with me?"

I smiled and nodded.

Chapter Fourteen

We walked back inside. Ella, Ivy, and Meryl came storming towards me. "Are you okay?" they cried.

"Girls, I appreciate the concern, but this night is not about me. Can we please enjoy it together?"

"Well, hello again, handsome, I'm Ivy," Ivy said, and extended her hand to Oliver.

"Yes," he said. "We've met. At least twice."

"God, you're cute." She reached for his hair as he gently denied her hand.

He laughed as Ella pulled on Ivy's dress, trying to tame her.

"Why isn't anyone dancing?" Ivy asked. "Come on, girls! You too, Oliver!"

Oliver grabbed my hand and led me to the dance floor. I looked at the piano player, and he shot me a wink, transitioning into *The Way You Look Tonight*. As he played the introduction, a woman in a gold dress came to stand behind him, swinging her hips to the music as she began singing: *"Someday when I'm awfully low, when the world is cold, I will feel a glow just thinking of you, and that way you look tonight."*

"You know who that pianist is, right?" Oliver asked me.

"No clue," I responded, watching the pianist handle the keyboard like a wizard.

"Stephen Kummer," Oliver said. "That's your fun fact for the day," he added as he spun me around. I laughed, feeling lightheaded from alcohol and emotion. I turned to see Meryl dancing and laughing with a man I didn't recognize. He was looking at her with an unmistakably starry-eyed expression as they swirled around together. She looked at me and I read her lips, *Ryan.* I gave her a thumbs up. Ivy was trying to dance a tango with Ella, Ella resisting. By the end of the tug-of-war, Ivy got her way. The two of them together were no different at an extravagant gala than in the living room of our apartment.

Later on the evening, the crowd began to dwindle, as did my energy. We were sauced up from the neverending catering service and champagne. Ella was ready to go; Meryl was saying her goodbyes; and Ivy had four men surrounding her at the bar as she gabbed about how much fun it was to work in PR. I motioned her, and she gave me a nod.

The four of us split a cab home.

"So Bobbie," Ivy said. "Give us the goods on sweet Oliver."

"He *is* sweet, isn't he?" I mused.

"If you ask me, he's way better than that guy Charlie."

"No one asked you," said Ella.

"So, Meryl," I said. "I saw you on the dance floor. Who was he?"

"I don't know who you're talking about!" she said and then smiled conspiratorially.

As we approached the building I now called home, I felt deep comfort with its antique beauty and rich history, as well as the personal history I was beginning to build there. The stories, laughs, and friendships that were unfolding inside were as rich, charming, and opulent as the building itself.

I noticed Barbara's living room light on. It was late in the evening, way past her usual bedtime, and I was a little worried. "You girls go ahead and go to bed. I'll check on Barbara." They yawned and nodded. I scurried up the stairs and lightly knocked on her door. "Barbara?"

I didn't hear a word, not even Due was doing his

usual run and greet routine. I twisted the old glass knob and the door creaked open. I poked my head in. It was silent and only the living room light was on. I stepped in, taking a look around. I didn't want to wake her, if she was asleep.

"Ahhh!" Barbara jumped out of the kitchen with a frying pan in her hand ready to attack.

"Barbara! It's me! It's just me!" I yelled in defense.

She dropped her arm and grabbed at her heart with her other hand. "Oh," she giggled, "I figured you were out for the night—thought you might be some man coming to get me!"

I shook my head. She truly was nutty. "We just got back from the gala. It was very glamorous, especially wearing this." I handed her the fur coat I had worn.

"Don't be ridiculous," she said, waving off the coat with a flick of her wrist. "I told you, it's yours! Tea?" I nodded my head happily, hoping all along she would be up and open to talk.

"Tell me be about your night. What a beautiful dress you're wearing!"

"Thank you, it was—interesting."

"How so?"

"Charlie showed with another girl, a model. It sucked at first, but then I stopped caring. It was almost a relief to see him with someone else. It made everything between us really over. I just feel bad for her, or the next girl who has to deal with his insecurities and shallowness. But who knows, maybe *she's* just like him. Maybe they're perfect for each other, and they'll live happily ever after."

"People are vain, Bobbie, baby." She motioned me to follow her into the kitchen, where she put the kettle on. "Vain in the sense that we're always trying to find the pieces in life that fit us. We're sifting and sifting, attempting to define ourselves. Thomas Merton once said, 'The beginning of love is the will to let those we love be perfectly themselves, the resolution not to twist them to fit our own image. If in loving them we do not love what they are, but only their potential likeness to ourselves, then we do not love them: we only love the reflection of ourselves we find in them.' The mind has an amazing ability to twist everything that exists into exactly as we want to see it. This is why you need to surround yourself with people who see clearly and defend that clarity with all your heart."

"I feel lucky in that regard," I said. "I have great friends I've had for years, like Meryl, and..." I thought of Oliver, and a strange warm tingling feeling filled me from head to toe, as I remembered how handsome he looked tonight. How good he smelled. And how charmed I'd been when he'd tucked his warm coat around me. "And now I have my crazy roommates, and I have you!"

When the kettle began to sing, Barbara filled two cups and dropped tea bags into both. "Bobbie," she said, "Do you remember when we talked about the three kinds of love?"

"Eros, Philia, and Agape, right?" I said. "Yes. But we only got as far as Eros!"

"Well, Philia is love in the form of friendship. It's the friendship you form with yourself and others. Even in romantic relationships, when the flame of Eros is no long able to shine, it is Philia that keeps couples together. Because at the end of the day, you still have to like yourself and your mate. Friendship, above all things, my love, lasts an eternity...beyond this life. It is Philia that suffuses, that fills every space in us, and turns all aggression to dust. Martin Luther King said that," she added.

I felt a lump in my throat; she looked deep into me, making me feel more vulnerable than ever. My eyes began to well.

"Thank you, Barbara. I think you are an angel."

"My husband used to say that. It's funny...you

remind me of him sometimes. You have the same kind eyes," she smiled. "And he was very shy, too, when he was a young man. Bobbie, you know that time goes by so quickly. Squeeze the life out of every moment, and when love finds you, never let go."

When I got back to my apartment, my phone buzzed with a text from Oliver.

I'm here if you need me.

Philia? Is that what Oliver and I have? I wondered. Friendship was certainly the foundation of our relationship. Yes, we definitely had some Philia going on. But if I was completely honest with myself, I had to admit that lately, where Oliver was concerned, Eros was coming into play as well. And I found that a bit... alarming. Oliver, *sexy?* I hadn't thought of him in that way since—well, never! So why now?

And what should I do about it?

Nothing. Nothing. Everyone knows the quickest way to kill a great friendship is to...to turn it into something more. Right? And what I had with Olly was just too important to risk—I couldn't, wouldn't jeopardize our friendship.

That night I tossed and turned. I got up out of bed to get a glass of orange juice, came back to my room and sipped it in the dark. *I'm going to start studying for the LSAT. I'm going to apply to law school. I'm going to quit Fordham. I'm going to ask Oliver what's going on in his head when he looks at me with that mysterious expression in those deep green eyes of his...*

In the middle of the night, things are so clear. But I knew by morning I'd change my mind again. I'd stay in my shell.

Chapter Fifteen

It was the morning of Fordham Agency's biggest day—the Centennial. You could think of the Centennial as the Super Bowl of the modeling industry. It was exclusive parties all day long, photo shoots at the hottest locations in the city, and in the evening, a runway show with all the top designers and top models, followed by a very exclusive after-party. Every inch of the agency had been glitterized; constant rehearsals on runways had been perfected; designer clothing filled the racks. All the studio spaces had been staged for exclusive photo shoots, and everyone affiliated with the Fordham agency had been called to action.

It was 7:30 a.m., and I awoke in a panic. What happened to my alarm clock? Late! And I had been doing so much better with that...

I threw on my fishnets, black dress, fur coat, and Jeffrey Campbells, not bothering with my hair, which was tied up in the messy knot I'd slept in and actually looked pretty chic. I ran out the door and down the street to the nearest coffee shop, iPad in one hand and purse in the other.

Businessmen stood against the walls reading the *Financial Times* and *Wall Street Journal,* waiting for double foam, double shot skim lattes.

"Double espresso please," I said, reaching into my purse to find my wallet and cell phone. I needed to arrange drivers for my foreign models who were currently staying at the Drake Hotel and the Hilton. After that I had to check all international flights coming into O'Hare. It was officially one of the biggest days of my career as an agent and I felt numb, running on an hour of sleep. I look like a zombie, I thought, as I caught a glimpse of myself in the pastry glass case.

Wallet, check. Phone? I searched and searched, digging through my bag. *Shit! It's on the nightstand.*

I downed the espresso on the sprint back home, and by the time got there, I was sweating in my fur, despite the fact that the weather was cold and stormy. I felt the caffeine activate; my hands almost trembled as I opened the front door.

Ella was doing yoga on the living room floor; Ivy was on the couch eating Fruit Loops and watching the news. *"Delayed flights: Delta, United, American Air, Lufthunsa, Air Italia..."*

"Forgot my phone," I breathlessly, as if they cared.

In my room, my phone was buzzing and lighting up: *New Text Message from* LILLY THE INTERN: *Trouble in paradise. Get to the office ASAP.*

This cheery communication was followed by six missed calls from Wolfe's secretary and three models. Was there a death? I wondered. Before calling Wolfe back, I tried to prepare myself for the urgency. I called Lilly. "What's going on?" I asked.

"Do you not read the news? Hurricane Sandy?"

"Yeah, what about it?"

"All flights at US airports are totally screwed up. Which means half our models won't be here for the Centennial shoot."

"Shit! I'll be there in ten minutes."

Half our models? *Half our models?*

I hung up and sprinted out to the living room, headed for the door. I had my hand on the handle when I was struck with a bolt of lightning—a brilliant idea. Stopped in mid-flight. I pivoted. I looked at Ivy and then at Ella.

At the serious expression on my face, Ivy's eyes grew rounded and huge, her mouth full of Fruit Loops.

"What?" Ella cried.

"Girls," I said. "How would you like to do me a *huge* favor?"

Ella shrugged. "Be glad to, if I can."

Ivy swallowed her cereal. "What?" she asked.

"Have you ever fantasized about being a model?"

"Of course," said Ella. "We're girls, aren't we? Once, with the Joffrey, we did this modern dance piece that was like a riff on the whole fashion industry—"

"Perfect," I said. "You're experienced. Ivy, you're a natural. Half our models have been grounded by Hurricane Sandy, and if you can step in and help me out, you'd be lifesavers."

Ivy opened her mouth full of rainbow Fruit Loops. "Oh my God! You're serious."

"Oh, no..." Ella shook her head. "No. I'm not...I'm not tall enough. Not nearly."

Well, I may be shy, but when it comes to recruiting talent, I'm no pushover. I refused to take no for an answer. "Reschedule with work. Call in sick. Do whatever you have to do," I said. "Get yourselves ready on the double and be ready when I call you."

I ran into the street to hail a cab, nearly getting hit by a biker, a car, and the yellow cab I finally hailed. "Fordham Agency," I cried. "Go! Go! Go!"

On the street, leaves were swirling and huge raindrops spattered the windshield of the cab. There was a lot of traffic, and we crawled slowly along. I should have just walked, I thought.

I burst through the glass doors at the agency. It smelled like hairspray. I could already hear Wolfe yelling, as desperate secretaries scurried around. Phones were ringing, and someone was already crying. *Jesus.*

Lilly popped out of my office. "Oh thank God you're here! Prepare yourself for this..." She grabbed my arm, dragging me to Wolfe's office. As the door swung open, there he was, standing in the middle of the room, throwing a temper tantrum. His platinum-perfect hair was a mess. He was pacing back and forth, yelling into the phone. Looking up at me as I came through the door, he hung up the phone and threw it across the room. It reminded me of when I threw Charlie's phone at his face. Not attractive.

"Bobbie, we're short six of your international models," he said.

"I know."

"Not to mention we are missing a photographer, a videographer, and two makeup artists."

"I was thinking I could—"

"Whatever it is, you have three hours to pull it off. In the meantime, I don't want to see you. Go!" he said, flipping his hand, shooing me away like a fly.

"I'm on it," I said.

"Then what are you still *doing* here?" he asked coldly.

Lilly was waiting for me outside. "Oh my God," she said. "He's terrifying!"

"Calm down and follow me. I need you," I told her. Back in my office, I called Ivy and Ella, then I opened every file cabinet in the room and threw Lilly an iPad. "I need you to go through all of the models in documents A, B, and C. Call two models, one female and one male from each, tell them all to report here by 11:30 for hair and make-up. After that, call the designers Paul and Pierre."

"Last names?"

"Paul and Pierre? Lilly, are you kidding me? It's like—Prince, you know, there's no last name, just call. Tell them it's an emergency and you're calling on behalf of Bobbie Bertucci."

Lilly's bug blue eyes stared at me, her face pale and drained.

"Did you get that, Lilly?"

She nodded.

"Okay, then hop to it!" I clapped my hands and she snapped out of her trance.

"Hey," I called after her. "It's all going to be okay!"

She nodded, color slowly returning to her face. I had her dial extra drivers to pick up the models, including Ella and Ivy, and I personally attempted to call Oliver six times. I couldn't believe he wasn't already part of Centennial. On second thought, yes—I could believe it. He had seemed so detached. So ready to move on. Well, maybe he'd be willing to come back for me.

The morning's craziness continued to escalate. It was terrifically cold, rainy, and there was absolutely no sun. I had never taken the time to venture into Wicker Park, but today I was desperate. I had to find him.

The cab pulled up in front of an old brick apartment building, the bottom level of which was an indie-type coffee shop. *He would,* was all I could think. I sprinted to the door, hit the doorbell three times and listened for noise on the other side. Nothing. I banged three times, putting my ear up to the door. My ears hurt, and I couldn't feel my fingers. *Bang, bang, bang!* I gave it three more whacks. Silence. I turned around and slid my body down the door, defeated. Suddenly, I felt the door give way, and I tumbled backwards. I laid flat on my back, looking up to see a girl hovering over me in a baggy Blink-182 T-shirt... and nothing else, as I could plainly see from my unique vantage point. Not even underwear. I scrambled to my feet, pulling my hair out of my mouth.

"Uh, hello!" I put my hand out for a shake. She stared. I put my hand back at my side. She looked cracked-out, hung-over, her black make-up smudged and her blonde hair a bird's nest. I'll admit her anorexic body and chiseled bone structure was a bit rocker chic, though. She squinted against the sky's overcast glare.

"Is Olly—is Oliver home?" I asked.

"No," she said.

"Do you know where I can find him?"

"No."

"Okay then," I crossed my arms. "Maybe I should wait for him."

"Are you that Robbie chick?" she asked.

"Bobbie."

"Yeah, yeah, Olly mentioned you." She sounded amused.

Well, *I'm* amused, too, I thought, feeling seriously grumpy and displeased by the turn of events. I mean, couldn't he do better than this? I knew Oliver was into the whole artsy, hipster-chick thing with girls, but still, this one just didn't seem his type.

"We hit it pretty hard last night, and I think he lost his phone or cracked it, or something," she said. "Oh wait, maybe that was *my* phone. I don't know. You can wait inside if you want. It's cold as shit out here."

I heard footsteps come pounding up the steps behind me, and I turned to see Oliver carrying a brown bag and two coffees.

"Bobbie!" He looked startled to see me, and a blush spread over his cheeks. "What's up? Uh—Lottie, Bobbie," he said by way of introduction, nodding at each of us in turn.

"Yeah, I kinda figured it out," Lottie said.

"Nice to meet you, Lottie. Olly, I *really* need to talk to you."

"Okay..." He thought a moment. "You should go back inside, Lot. Maybe put on some real clothes? I'll be in there in a minute." Oliver took the girl by the shoulders and turned her around, pushing her in through the door, which he closed carefully behind her. He turned around and looked at me. "Hi."

"Hey," I said hesitantly. I felt mortified. I had just walked in on Oliver with a morning-after girl!

"She's um...that's actually my cousin, Lottie," he said, and scratched his head. "That probably looked really bad."

"Oliver, it's okay. You don't have to lie about it. Not to me."

"No really, she's my cousin. I promise. She was going to school in Boston, but she dropped out, and she doesn't want to go home. She's having a lot of problems, as you can see from her hot mess of an appearance."

"Olly, I believe you," I assured him, with an offhand shrug. *No big deal.* But inside I felt incredibly relieved. Lottie, his cousin. *Right.* He had talked about his cousin Lottie over the years, but I'd never met her before today.

"Okay then," he sighed, and relaxed his shoulders. We stood there for a moment looking at each other. "Coffee?" He bent down and picked up a steaming cup. "I've got scones too."

"Oliver, the real reason I'm here is—" I took a deep breath.

"What?" I watched as his eyes lit up. I swear he suddenly looked hopeful.

"Hurricane Sandy."

"Huh?" He frowned.

"Hurricane Sandy caused a million flight delays, creating havoc with Centennial. Long story short, I desperately need a good photographer in order to make points with Wolfe and make Ivy and Ella look like professional models who know what they're doing."

"Oh."

"Can you? Would you?" I put my hands together, bending my knees, praying he'd say yes.

"For the Centennial," he said flatly

I nodded in confirmation.

"Runway or set shoot?"

"Probably both, but I'm really not sure yet..."

"Okay. Let me change and grab my equipment."

"You're my hero!" I yelped. Impulsively I grabbed him in a hug. He hugged me back, but just briefly, stiffly, then he pushed me away.

I followed him into his flat. We climbed a flight of stairs, and the room opened up into a large white loft. The white walls were covered with giant blow-ups of his photos, and an enormous old-fashioned clock hung on a brick wall above mahogany shelves filled with hundreds of books. Two beautiful guitars were mounted by a window with views of the city. The furniture was leather, and the wood floors were strewn with sheepskin rugs. Lottie was curled up in a chair, flipping through a magazine.

"Want some coffee or vodka or something?" she asked.

"Oh, no thanks," I said. "I'm uh...working." For a moment I actually considered recruiting Lottie, adding her to my emergency stable of models, but then I thought better of it.

I walked over to look at some Polaroid pictures pinned on a board made of wine corks, and my heart did a flop to see that half of them were photos of me. There was one of me in a new white suit, just before I started my job at Fordham. I had felt so excited and hopeful that day! There were prom pictures, like the one of Oliver and me pretending to pick each other's noses. And another one of me sitting drunk in my prom dress crying because I dropped cake on my dress. How I had loved that dress. Then there we were, dancing at one of the many music festivals we'd attended together...

"Ready?" He snuck up behind me with his camera bag around his shoulder.

"Ready."

We said goodbye to Lottie and started down the stairs.

"Careful out there," she called. "I heard there's going to be a big storm."

We made our grand entrance together through Fordham Agencies' big glass doors. "Oliver, good to see ya back, buddy!" said one of the graphic designers as he cut past us, patting Oliver on the shoulder.

"Hi Olly," squeaked one of the secretaries.

"Welcome back, Oliver," purred a half-naked model with long platinum hair.

He gave a nod and a smile to all. Most people would be puffed up with ego at the attention he was getting lately, but Oliver remained completely unaffected. He merely returned the warm embrace the office seemed to give to him.

We went to the studio where racks of clothing awaited the professional models who would never come.

"Well," I said out loud, looking down at my phone. "That was Jen. She's doing video. Ivy and Ella are on their way. The car is dropping them off at the set. So... it's all coming together."

Hair dresser and make-up artist Stefania popped her head around the corner. She was wearing a black turtleneck, her hair short like Twiggy, and purple lipstick.

"Bobbie, we're ready for you," she informed. "You have to get in for hair and make-up in the next thirty minutes. I saved you a spot, and your outfit is hanging in your office. I got you the cheetah jacket."

"Yep, thanks. One sec," I replied.

"So, Bobbie," said Olly, pointing down the hall. "I'll just—"

"Yes, please, go! Thank you!" I blew him a kiss and ran to my office. Lilly was talking on the phone, sitting in my chair with her feet up on my desk.

She hopped up. "Sorry!"

"Pretending to be an agent?" I asked.

"Ye-yeah."

"Keep your feet off my desk. What's the word?"

"I contacted all the models you told me to contact ,and we're pretty much able to get at least half of them here in the next hour for hair and makeup."

"Pretty much able or able?"

"Able."

"Great," I said. "Good job. Can you list the names, please?"

"Sure," she sighed dramatically. "Women: Ariel Truman, Danielle Munson, Alessandra Valentino..." Lilly looked up at me.

"Okay, great, Lilly. And how about the men?" I

asked, as I opened a drawer and grabbed my phone charger.

"Well, she said. "I don't think you're going to like this."

I knelt to plug the charger in under my desk. "I won't like what?"

Lilly sighed again. "All I've got so far is Chance Brooks."

I reared up too quickly, hitting my head on my desk. *Charlie.* Dear God. "Excuse me," I said. "Did you say Chance Brooks? Wasn't he already booked?"

"No, that was cancelled. Anyway, he's the only one I could get a hold of. I tried others but he was the only one available, at least so far!" When she saw my expression, she cringed. I wanted to throw her out the window.

"I'm sorry," she said.

It's not her fault. It's not her fault. I continued to chant it to myself, hoping to lower my skyrocketing blood pressure. "It's okay, Lilly. Thank you. I'm going to make-up now..."

After spending twenty-five minutes in hair and make-up, I called a driver to escort Lilly and me over to the set where they were shooting a 1970s rock theme on the roof of Vertigo Sky Lounge. It was my job to make sure that everything was playing out accordingly and up to Wolfe's standards.

We pulled up at Vertigo Sky Lounge; I grabbed Lilly's hand and we ran in, jumping into the elevator that would take us to the rooftop. I walked onto the set where one of my last-minute makeup artists was putting the finishing touches on one of my last-minute models.

"Sewing kit!" I yelled to Lilly. "Lilly?" I turned to see her flirting with one of the male models. "Lilly!" I yelled to her. She ran over, rummaging through the bag that was heavier than she was. I quickly stitched a rip in my model's costume, and we spent a total of thirty-three minutes at the 1970s shoot. I texted our driver, and we were off to the next stop, catching our breath in the car. Lilly studied the mini-bar, picking up a little bottle of scotch.

"Don't even think about it."

"Oh c'mon. You're no fun," she pouted.

"Lilly, we're working, not playing," I said.

Lilly rolled her eyes. "I know. I was only joking."

We pulled up to our destination, a reinvented Union Station in a warehouse: Chicago in the 1950s. I was excited to see how this one had turned out because the 1950s were my favorite era. I was blown away by the incredible set the designers had created. The models looked great, hanging out of the fake train. One of the designers started yelling at a model, warning her not to pull on the props. Turns out that model was Ivy. She was in the train with Ella, and they were both clearly having a blast. They looked fantastic, too. The makeup artist had transformed them into 50s starlets.

Suddenly there was Oliver, walking toward me with his easy stride.

"Olly!" Ordinarily I would be running up to him, giving him a hug. But for some reason, at that moment, I held back. "Are you shooting all this?" I asked.

"Yup, I guess so," he said humbly. "This is my favorite set by far."

"Mine too."

"Your friends look great," he said. "Your roommates, anyway."

I glanced over at the models. I tested my feelings as my eyes found Charlie. He was acting pretty chummy with Alessandra, his date from the gala. She was dressed in a vintage skirt and blazer, with a beige leather briefcase and a hat she kept waving from the window of the train. She looked phenomenal with deep red lipstick in contrast with her pale skin. Charlie looked thinner than usual and—could it be there were bags under his eyes?

I took a deep breath and walked over. "Everything going okay here?"

Ivy and Ella waved and laughed; Charlie slid his arm around Alessandra's tiny waist.

"All is well. Thanks, Bobbie," Alessandra said sweetly. "That's a great coat, BTW."

"Thanks. I got it from a real 50s pinup girl." I winked at Ivy and Ella.

"Really? How cool."

"So, roomies—thank you so much for doing this!"

"You owe us," Ivy said. "I'll take my payment in a bottle of champagne. Make it two!" I walked closer to the girls, almost wishing I could join them.

"I've never been around so many gorgeous guys," Ella whispered. "Am I sweating?"

"No, you look great. You both do!" I said.

"I always look great," Ivy said a little louder. "This guy knows what I'm talking about." The male model just looked at her, then cracked a smile.

"She may have had few drinks before we came here. Even Ivy gets nervous," Ella said under her breath.

"Okay, well just keep an eye on her," I said to Ella. But from the looks of it, people were finding Ivy rather entertaining. I just prayed it would stay that way.

I found Lilly at a large table piled with low-calorie snacks and bottled water. Watching her gobble at least one of everything on the table, I was tempted to pour the bottle of water on her head. "On to the next shoot!" I yelled, grabbing her hand. I waved goodbye to everyone on the set, trying to avoid looking at Charlie.

"Hey, Bobbie. Wait up!" I turned around to see Oliver running towards me.

"Do you want me to develop these photos in the dark room, back at the agency?" he asked. "Or should I use my own studio?"

"It's up to you," I said. "But you might as well use the agency's equipment..."

"I'm busy all day tomorrow, but I was thinking after work tomorrow night."

"Sure. Whatever works for you."

"Great," Oliver smiled. "I'll call you."

"Okay!" I grabbed Lilly's arm as we ran toward the car. My heart was pounding, and it wasn't just from the exertion.

"You were super awkward just then," Lilly said, looking at me laughing.

"What? No, I wasn't," I said.

"Oh yes, you were," she snorted.

"Listen, you do not talk to your boss like that. Do you understand?" I said, shutting her up. "You need to remember you're an intern, and—" But my authoritative tone fell apart, and I started laughing. I just felt so happy all of a sudden.

"Meow!" she said.

"Get in the car," I commanded, pushing her in by her head.

The next stop was the old Chicago Fire Station where the set was reenacting the great Chicago fire. The minute we got to the set, one of the assistants ran up to inform me that one of my models had food poisoning.

"Is it serious? Where is she?" I asked. "You guys are an hour behind schedule."

"She's in the bathroom," the assistant told me with worried eyes. Probably scared he'd be fired.

"Lilly," I said, "Alka-Seltzer and Pepto Bismol!" I ran to the bathroom, shoved medication down the model's throat and made her drink ginger ale. I called in hair and makeup to fix her in the bathroom and had a photographer take a few photos, because she *did* look rather chic, curled around the vintage toilet.

"Nice work," I encouraged her. "You're a true artist."

"Mmm...hmm," the model nodded miserably. The

poor frail girl stood up and dragged herself back to the set. I overheard her telling one of the other models she was thrilled she'd puked up everything she'd eaten the past few days.

I stood back and watched the photo shoot, trying to catch my breath.

"A little tough on model-girl, weren't you?" A voice with a thick accent spoke from behind me.

"Excuse me?" I turned.

He was dressed far too casually for the high-end style of the shoot, in khaki pants, a white button-down shirt that hung loosely on his rock solid body, and shoes that looked like they could've been made out of hemp. His hair was long, down to his shoulders, and golden from lots of exposure to the sun. He looked me in the eye. "The girl's puking her cookies, and you send her back into the fire rather than home with a cup of soup?"

"Just trying to do my job," I said. *Who was this guy?*

"Nah, I can respect it. Just a little tough," he added with a laugh, crossing his arms, watching the photo shoot. "I'm Zander," he said.

"Bobbie," I offered my hand.

He accepted it, but said, "You Americans, so formal with your handshake. And isn't Bobbie a boy's name?"

"Bobby with a Y is a boy's name. I'm Bobbie with an i-e."

"Okay, then, American Bobbie with an i-e," he laughed.

"Don't you have nicknames where you come from? My name is actually Roberta. So, what's your role here?"

"I'm the set designer, graphic designer—well, designer in general, I guess. Fordham paid me a boatload of money to come do this, so I thought, why not? Never been to Chicago before, but I gotta say it's really not my cup of tea. Like, where's the sun? You've got great eyes."

I blushed. "As a Chi-town girl, I apologize for my city. The weather has been absolutely lousy."

"Apology accepted. So, what's there to do in this town, anyway? Like, nightlife?" He brushed back his hair. "Like I said, I'm not from around these parts. As if you couldn't tell." He grinned at me. I was finding his accent more and more attractive.

"Where are you from?" I asked.

"New Zealand. Ever been?"

I shook my head no.

"Ah, it's a great place, beautiful scenery, nice people, great beaches. You have to visit sometime," he smiled.

"I'd like that. And as far as nightlife here in Chicago, there's an after-party tonight at Fordham following the runway show..."

"You gonna be there?"

"I am."

"Great. So I'll see you there?" he looked at me for confirmation.

"Yeah. I'll be there."

"Great. It was great meeting you hazel-eyed American Bobbie with an i-e. I'll see you when the sun's down." He motioned towards the set.

"Go do your job," I smiled.

"All right then," he said and went back to work. Lilly came up behind me, draping her arm around my shoulder.

"Who was that foxy man with the accent?" she asked, bumping her hip against mine.

"Zander, the designer, from New Zealand," I said.

"Well? Did you get that hottie's number or what?" she asked, with a mouthful of something.

"What are you eating? You're always eating!"

"Free miniature muffins. Hey, the models aren't eating them. I might as well. Want one?" She lifted her hand, holding out three more muffins.

"No, thank you. Where do all those calories go? I thought you told me you didn't use food as anesthesia, Lilly. And here you are scarfing everything in sight, when you're not trying to break into the mini bar in the car—"

"Yeah, but that's like, for *fun*."

"But this is work," I said. "I know, I know. Work can be fun, though, you know...I do want to thank you for your help today, Lilly," I said. "You do at least keep things entertaining."

"Aww...is ice cold Bobbie Bertucci warming up to Lilly?" she said in a baby voice.

"Why are you talking in third person?" I said. "Come on. We still have a lot of work to do."

She snorted. "Yeah, you're all right too," she said, and popped another muffin in her mouth.

Everywhere I turned that night, I saw someone I knew. Everyone from work was there, including Lilly, all my local models, those who had been able to fly in, and those I'd recruited. Ivy and Ella strutted into the after-party in the highest heels they owned. Ivy told anyone who would listen that she was now a Fordham model. Charlie was there—but not with Alessandra. Oliver came with his cousin Lottie, who had cleaned up pretty well and seemed to be behaving herself. My boss Wolfe was there, of course, and when I saw him approaching me, I thought he might be coming over to compliment me on a job well-done. We had pulled off the event in fine style, despite the crisis. I knew it was largely due to my resourcefulness and energy in filling the gaps with so many of my colleagues and friends who had generously stepped up to help us out. But I was dreaming if I thought Wolfe had any sense of gratitude or the ability to express such a thing as appreciation. He merely informed me that he needed the red lace dress back.

"Make sure it's hanging on the rack in the studio by 8 a.m.," he said. "Cleaned and pressed."

He turned away without another word. I just glared after him. The fact that he didn't complain was compliment enough for me. I couldn't expect any more than that. I knew better, but couldn't help but feel underappreciated.

"Hey, roomie," Ella said. She appeared at my side. "You look..."

"Are you okay?" Ivy popped up between us. "Who is that man you look like you want to throw your drink on?"

"That's my soon-to-be-ex-boss."

"Oh, wow—really? Wait...*ex-boss?*"

"Really. Girls, I want you to be the first to know. I am officially giving my notice. I am going to apply for law school."

"Did I just hear you say law school?" Oliver poked his head between Ivy and Ella.

"Yep," I said. "It's official. I'm gonna do it."

"Well, Jesus. It's about time," he said.

"Yay!" Ivy held her glass high. "To Bobbie Bertucci, attorney at law!"

"Yeah, to keep you out of jail, Ivy," I said. "But shh, I don't want my boss to hear. Not yet. I have to get my ducks in a row before I can quit."

Wolfe hadn't heard Ivy's toast, but Charlie did. He actually squeezed his way into our little group. Before I realized what was happening, he had slid his arm around me, saying, "Oh God, you're not rehashing that old law school fantasy again, are you, Bertucci?" He chuckled. "Really, I would think you'd be embarrassed to say these things out loud. You know it's a lot of work and actual reading, honey. Law school is like, you know, *school*."

"I understand school and working hard isn't a concept you get, Charlie," I said, staring him dead in the eye. He had nothing else to say and slinked away.

"Wow," Ella said. "What a charmer! Lucky you got

out when you did. He obviously can't be happy for other people."

"I wouldn't expect him to be," I said. "He once told me I'd never be able to pass the LSAT, let alone the bar."

Ivy wrinkled her nose. "The *what?*"

"Bobbie," Ella said, "I think you'll make a great lawyer. You have a knack for finding out the truth in people."

I had expected Oliver would chime in with what he usually said whenever I broached the subject of law school: "But of course. It's totally your calling, Bobbie," he'd say. "It's the perfect career for you—getting paid to argue!" But he didn't say it this time—because he had already wandered off. When I finally spotted him through the crowd, he was dancing with one of the models from the agency who'd been hitting on him for months now.

Zander showed up, still underdressed, but he was so good-looking he had no problem pulling it off. He asked me to dance, and we had a great time, dancing, laughing and drinking together. He was a great hit with Ivy and Ella.

I was hoping Oliver might ask me to dance, too, but he had vanished. I didn't see him the rest of night.

I didn't know how I felt since he'd left so abruptly. I brushed it off, but knew on some level it annoyed me. But I was over letting boys determine how my night went. The cards were in my hands now. My roommates were having the time of their lives, so I decided to join them. If I had learned one thing, it was that your girl friends were the people you could count on time and again. They were the other pieces of my puzzle holding me together. I was thankful for that. We stayed out to till the sun came up having a night we'd never forget.

Chapter Sixteen

The next evening I met Oliver at Fordham to let him in, as he no longer had his own access. We were making our way to the darkroom, and as we rounded a corner, I found myself trailing behind him, taking in his broad, muscular shoulders, his tapering back... He had a swimmer's body. His legs were long and strong. He suddenly turned back and looked at me. "I probably should have done this in my new studio, but I figured we might as well use Wolfe's..." He grinned, and I quickly lifted my gaze to meet his, hoping he hadn't caught me checking him out.

We had reached the dark room. I unlocked the door.

"Want to see what we've got?" he asked.

I nodded.

He opened the double doors and out came a waft of pungent chemicals.

"This is it." There was a buzzing noise before the

red lights came on. In the center of the room was an island topped with square trays. Around the perimeter of the room were the booths with the machines in them. Streams of photos clipped to a wire hung from the ceiling.

I said in a low voice, "I feel like I'm in a horror movie."

"Don't worry babe. I'll protect you!"

I laughed as I slowly walked along, studying the hanging photos and the marvels of anorexic high-end models.

"So, what we're doing is developing 35MM film," he said. "First thing we do is rewind so we can take it out of the camera." He began furiously twisting a knob on the top of his camera. "We're going to develop it, hang it, then take it into the handy-dandy private lab where we'll use the enlarger..."

As dorky as he was in that moment, it was kind of hot watching him in his element.

"So we can use the Patterson tank here, which is just a little tank into which we put our 35MM reel with our chemicals or we can tray process. First thing, tray process." He handed me a pair of gloves.

"We lay the sheets carefully into the tray, giving it a little bath like so...." He slid his arm around my waist and pulled me in front of him. "Try it," he said. I swallowed hard as felt the warmth of his body against mine. He showed me how to flip and 'agitate' the film.

"There," I said. "Agitated enough?"

"Definitely," he replied.

I took a deep breath. It was getting hot in this small room.

"After this, we give our film a bath."

Watching him show me his world with such expertise and enthusiasm was entertaining—not to mention extremely sexy.

"We set it into a tank which prevents all light from entering, and wash it in water..." he continued talking, throwing out terminology I'd never heard before. "... because D70-6 solution is the..." I was no longer listening to what he was saying. I had become way more intent upon the nearness of his body. It was like a magnetic pull.

"There we go, freshly exposed black and white film."

He loaded the film around the wheel, smoothly and gracefully, treating it with great care. "So, are you still seeing Charlie?" he asked suddenly, jarring me out of my sensual trance. "Now, put the film in the tank," he went on, without waiting for me to answer, and he plopped it into a small canister. "Chemicals." He smiled and poured in a potent smelling liquid.

"You look like a mad scientist," I said, "flipping the canister of film, pouring liquid here, dumping it there."

"Now, the film is washed and ready." He put his hands on his hips, and he looked into my eyes. He held my gaze.

I could hear the blood pumping in my ears.

"Well?" he asked.

"Fascinating," I said. "Watching you."

"He's not good enough for you, Bobbie."

Without thinking I stepped towards him, and leaning in, I touched his chest. He didn't move, and I could hear his breath in the quietness. I closed my eyes, and lifted my head just a little, hoping to feel his soft lips against mine.

One moment passed, then another.

But nothing happened. I opened my eyes, he was looking down at me, and then—at the photos.

I stepped back, afraid. "Oh," I uttered, "Olly—I'm—ugh—sorry."

"For?" He began to reorganize the film in the tray. My heart sank.

He moved past me to the laundry wire, unclipped a few photos and handed them to me.

"Here, you may want to review these. They're the ones I already developed earlier today."

"I didn't know you came earlier. I thought you were busy."

"I finished early and came over. Joey let me in."

I risked a glance at him, but he wouldn't look at me. The silence was awkward, and my heart raced. *How did I completely misread him?* I was so embarrassed. Everyone was wrong. He didn't like me. How did I not see it? I shifted my gaze, looking down at the photos. Scanning through them quickly I realized most of them were photos of Charlie.

Oliver looked away and made himself busy. "So, I still have quite a few of these to do tonight...you don't have to stick around," he added, dipping film in the tray.

Was that his way of asking me to leave?

"Okay, then..." I took off my gloves, throwing them in a trash bin. "I'll leave you to it." He gave me a nod. I walked out the door with tears in my eyes. I stood outside the darkroom for a moment, pacing back and forth, wondering if I should go back in and apologize or if I should swing open the door, grab him and kiss him. I banged my head against the wall, turning and covering my mouth, mortified, as the moment replayed in my head.

I thought of how Ivy wouldn't have taken no for an answer. She would've turned around and charged in there and made it happen. Me? I'm a crab, and I retreated into my shell. I hurried to the elevator, pressing the button a hundred times as I waited impatiently. *Get me out of here!*

I walked out of the building, my head woozy from the smell of chemicals. At first I thought I was hallucinating when I heard someone yelling my name. I recognized the accent before I saw the face. I turned to see buff and beautiful kiwi man, jogging towards me, his hair flopping on his shoulders.

"Zander, what are you still doing here? It's late!"

He stopped to catch his breath and brush back his hair. "Get a drink with me, will you?" He asked. And I wasn't about to turn him down.

"Okay."

We walked to a bar around the corner. He seemed quieter, shyer than he'd been at the after-party. Did I make him nervous? His accent was by far the sexiest thing about him. I couldn't get enough of it, as he leaned over the bar ordering our drinks from the bartender—a beer for him, pinot noir for me.

"Liking Chicago?" I asked.

"Better now," he flirted. He was so light-hearted, and his life seemed filled with adventure and intensity. He spoke of his spiritual experience when he hiked the Kakoda Trail in the mountains of New Guinea. He made it sound like a mythical fairy land, like a place you'd only dream about. He made me want to escape, with his free-bird approach to life.

"There is no better place than New Zealand. It's green for miles and miles, and the locals are the nicest people you'll ever meet," he said winking at me.

"Really? I've only met one New Zealander, and he was kind of boring," I teased.

"Impossible!" He retorted as he moved closer to me.

But as he talked, I realized I was treating him like Olly. Then I realized I wished he was Olly. I couldn't get my mind off what had happened. I didn't know what was going on. Why did I come on to him like that? Why did he reject me? Did he reject? Was I high off the fumes? Was that what made me want to touch him? What was he thinking right now?

I needed to admit to myself. I wanted to be with Oliver. I can't believe I was fighting it this whole time. Why hadn't I realized it before?

"Bobbie?" Zander's voice cut through my reverie.

"Hey, you look like you're a million miles away."

I snapped back into it. "You're right. I'm sorry. There is somewhere I need to be," I said. Zander was a great guy, and I would have loved to get to know him better. But tonight, my mind was full of Oliver.

I grabbed my coat and walked back towards Fordham, hoping I might catch Oliver on his way out of the building, or still in the darkroom.

My phone buzzed. Speak of the devil. "Where are you?" Oliver asked.

"Where are *you*?" I asked.

"Bobbie, I'm sorry."

"No, I'm sorry."

"Meet me at our spot?"

"Okay."

He hung up.

I shouldn't have come on to him like that, I kept telling myself. I had freaked him out. Now he wants to set things straight. Tell me it would never work. He likes me as a friend. That's all. I felt like such an idiot. I hailed a cab.

"Alfred Caldwell Lily Pool!" I said to the driver. It had been our favorite meeting spot since high school.

"The zoo's closed at this hour of night ma'am," the dark eyed driver stated.

"I'm aware!"

I bit my nails the whole way to the Lily Pool, when I wasn't playing with my necklace and fidgeting with my hair. *I'm a wreck! Pull yourself together, Roberta!* Why did I even care about what Oliver thought of me? I felt out of my element.

Then I thought about it. I had always cared about what Olly thought of me. Of all the opinions of all my friends, it was his I valued most. I rubbed my hands together nervously.

After throwing money at the cab driver, I leapt out of the car and ran towards the lily pool, hoping I'd see Oliver standing there waiting for me. As I whipped around the corner I slowed, attempting to catch my breath.

"Olly?" I looked around, but Oliver was nowhere to be found. My feet were killing me so I took off my shoes and ran barefoot, ruining the bottom of my tights. I sat down on a stone. Here, the city was silent, except for the hum of traffic from nearby Lake Shore Drive...and the sound of my own breath. My throat ached as I gasped in the cold air.

One minute went by.

Five minutes.

Ten minutes.

Sixteen minutes.

Where was he?

My hands were stiff. I blew into them. *C'mon Oliver.* I heard the thump of feet as he ran around the corner, coming to save the day.

"I was beginning to think you weren't going to show," I said darkly.

"But *I* asked *you* to meet me," he said. "You knew I'd show."

"I know. Listen, I'm so sorry about...what happened in the dark room. I think it must have been the fumes."

"The fumes? I hope not."

"But you..."

As I spoke, my cell phone slowly slipped from my ice cold hands. Oliver and I both went down for it at the same time, smacking heads. His mouth hit my forehead, and my forehead had no mercy on his mouth. "Ah!" I yelped, grabbing my head.

"Shit, Bobbie," he exclaimed. He licked his bottom lip, checking for blood.

"I'm really not trying to kill you," I cried, gently touching his face. "Are you bleeding?"

"Minor flesh wound," he said. We looked at each other and burst into laughter.

I guided him to sit down on the stone bench. I

covered my mouth trying to stop laughing, apologizing again.

He sighed. "Can we go back to talking about what happened in the darkroom and me rejecting you?"

"Rejection, ouch. Yes."

"Don't look at me like that," he said.

"Like what?"

He sat in silence, putting his head in his hands.

"Oliver, what's wrong?"

He looked up at me, as if in pain.

"Is it your lip?"

"No, Bobbie, it's not my lip," he said quietly.

"Then what is it?"

He sighed and looked out into the distance. He looked at me again. "Bobbie, honestly, do you know how hard it is to want someone, to want someone so badly and not be able to have them?"

He inhaled a large gulp of air. "No," he said, "you don't. Do you know what it's like when every time you see that person, you're different because they bring out the best in everyone?" He stared at me in the darkness.

What was going on? I didn't understand what he was trying to say. He couldn't be talking about me. I knew that much. I felt my stomach drop. Maybe it was

Lilly.

Looking down at his hands, he continued, "This is all really forward, but I can't take it anymore. You just need to know, Bobbie."

"Did I do something to upset you, Olly?" I asked softly. "If I did, I'm sorry."

"No, no, it's the exact opposite," he blurted.

"Talk to me." I touched his arm.

"Do you realize I've had to see you almost every day of my life since high school, and you've driven me nearly insane? I can't get enough of you. You're the only person I want to be around all the time. You bring out the best version of me—you always have. I see you sometimes, and I want to be the one who makes you laugh until you do that snort thing you can't control. I want to be the one who makes you happy. And I don't want to see you with some asshole who doesn't deserve you."

It was all pouring out now.

"I love that you laugh at me even when I'm not funny," he said. "I love that you laugh at your own jokes even when they aren't funny. I don't know what's going on with you lately, but I can't help but feel it's just the beginning of what it could be for us. There are so many more adventures in store for both of us. I want to go through them all with you. I want you, and I will wait for you to find whatever it is you're looking for, but I'm telling you…it's not here…" He poked my head with his finger. "It's here," he said, touching my chest, just above my sternum. His touch seemed to burn through my clothing.

"I'm afraid," he said. "You are the most amazingly beautiful person I've ever seen, and I don't know…"

He wasn't a poet, but he was honest and stronger than I was. I was blown away. I thought Olly had a crush on me, but it was much more than that. I realized that I thrived off his bravery. He was a solid rock, and I was liquid.

"I had no idea," I said.

"You don't know how bad it is," he said. "Why are you smiling?" he asked. "I'm being totally serious with you, Bobbie."

"I know, I know you are. But the way you're talking," I said, "it's crazy. I'm nothing special. In fact, I'm a mess. You know that better than anyone. I'm an emotional train wreck. I'm constantly second-guessing myself. I'm overly sensitive and flat-out insecure. I search and search for some kind of stable ground, but can't ever seem to find it. I'm vain and tend to care about things that don't really matter…"

He interrupted me. "Bobbie, don't you think I know you by now? If anything, you try far too hard. I know you do it all because you care and you worry, but you don't even realize what you're capable of." He gave me a strange look, scrunching his eyebrows and narrowing his eyes.

"You're not broken, Bobbie. You don't need to be fixed. And you don't have to be with someone who doesn't get you. You can do so much better than Charlie."

"Yes. I know."

"You...do?"

"Yes. Olly, I haven't been with Charlie since I moved into my new place."

"Really? But I thought...why didn't you tell me?"

"Maybe for the same reason you didn't tell me about the studio. I had to make sure I had the strength to make it stick."

"And did you? Have the strength, I mean?"

"I don't even need strength for it anymore," I said with a smile. "Because it's easy."

"It is?"

"Yes. What I need the strength for now, is...getting you to see that I—that I want..."

"You want?" he encouraged me softly.

"I want *you*, Oliver."

He looked down at me. All of a sudden there was no need for words. He wrapped his arms around me and brought me close. His lips smothered mine in the most gentle kiss. It was soft and tentative at first, but it quickly flared into something else entirely, becoming hungry and desperate, and it left us both breathless. It was strange, scary and exciting, but it felt like coming home.

My hands were numb. My ears, nose, and tips of my toes were ice, but my heart was racing hot. I looked up to see the clouds had parted right above us, and the stars were on fire. He looked up too.

"Remember when I used to make up the names of constellations?" I asked.

He laughed. "Yeah, like calling the big dipper Andromenapolous."

"I just did it to impress you, you know."

"Impress me? Really?"

"Uh huh." I laughed, blushing. I thought, *There is no other place in the world I'd rather be than sitting in the dark with him by my side.* "What would I do without you, Olly?"

"You'd probably find yourself in a white padded room in a straight jacket."

I pretended to take a swing at him, and he gently grabbed my hand. "Jesus, your hands are ice!"

"I know!"

"We better go."

"I don't want to go. I'm happy here. But I don't want you to get hypothermia."

He had his arms around me, trying to keep me warm. "Do you know the best way to take care of hypothermia?" he asked.

"How?"

"Naked body warmth," he said.

"Hmm. I wonder how we might arrange *that*?"

"I've got an idea."

I could hear his heart racing, the rhythm of the blood pumping through his veins thrilled me. My heart was sinking into the depths of the earth. It was the closest I'd ever been to crying tears of joy. My throat ached as I fought back my tears.

"You hear that?" he asked.

"Hear what?" I asked. "All I hear is your heartbeat."

"Listen, it's music."

"Mr. Prince, there's no music." I tried listening, but heard nothing but the wind.

He stood and extended his hand. "Dance with me, my princess." He smiled. "My *darling*."

Chapter Sixteen

I stood from the stone bench and took his warm hand. He twirled me around and pulled me close. "You're the one for me," his lips murmured against my hair.

We spent the rest of the evening walking, talking, hugging, kissing and talking some more until we both were hoarse. Finally, we ended up at my place. I would have invited him in. I wanted to, but I thought I had enough experience to know that I wanted our first time together to be something really special, and I was willing to wait.

Chapter Seventeen

Knock, knock.

"Morning, sleepy head!" Meryl poked her head in my bedroom door.

I growled. "What time is it?"

"I was thinking we could have a quick rooftop coffee together. Get up. Get up!"

"Okay, okay. Let me grab a blanket."

I crawled out of bed, snatched my plush throw, and we climbed up the stairs towards the steel door. On the terrace, we sat and sipped hot coffee—satisfying and warm in contrast with the frigid air.

"Something's different with you," Meryl said. "You have an odd look about you today...What is it?"

"Nothing at all. In fact...all is well. Very well."

"Bobbie!" she exclaimed. "What's going on?" She looked at me intently.

"It's nothing!" I yelled, but laughed. Every girl in the world had uttered that phrase and knew that "nothing" was always jammed packed with a lot of somethings. "Okay, so I'm lying."

"Is it...boy drama again?"

"Yep. I think you could say yes. Definitely."

"Oh, no, Bobbie...you didn't get back together with Charlie. Tell me you didn't..."

"No! God, no. It's...it's not Charlie."

"Then...is it Zander?"

"It's Oliver."

"Ohhhh...." She nodded knowingly. "Well it's about time." She murmered.

"Now, I know it hasn't been that long since Charlie and I broke up, and you probably think I should be single for awhile, you know, to get my own sense of self together, but...I really like him, Meryl, like really *really* like him."

"Bobbie."

"What?"

"I think it's great."

"You do?"

"I do. I love Oliver. He's one of the best guys I know. And I know he's crazy about you."

"He is? I mean, you know that? How do you know that?"

"It's obvious, Bobbie. I can see by the way he looks

at you."

Ahh...that warmed my heart, and made me think of something Barbara had said. *You'll know you have found him by the way he looks at you...*

"I'm really happy for you," she said, but not with real conviction.

"Thanks. But why am I not convinced?"

"Bobbie, don't take this the wrong way, but...I really didn't think you'd have the sense to go for a man like Oliver! I really thought you'd have to blow through a few more Charlies before you learned your lesson."

I burst out laughing. I felt a little insulted by her comment, but I had to admit, I understood it. "So, anyway," I said. "On to a more important topic. Are we all having dinner on the roof tonight?"

"You betcha. Barbara's infamous chicken cacciatore! Ella and Ivy are in charge of cocktails and wine. Do you want to take care of dessert?"

"Music to my ears. And taste buds. I'm thinking cheesecake. Ella's been dragging me to her dance classes, and my ass has never been tighter. I'm going to splurge."

"Dancing is the cure to everything."

"Yeah, you don't need to tell me. I've walked in on you during your solo Brazilian samba nights, you weirdo," I laughed, sipping my coffee.

"Don't make fun of me. I like to samba!"

"Well, that's great, 'cause if I have anything to say about it, we're gonna samba tonight." Meryl and I spent the rest of the morning chatting about her new beau and the guys waltzing in and out both Ella and Ivy's lives that seemed to change on a weekly basis. I had to say I was surprised. I realized that with all of my recent 911s in life, I had not taken the time to notice that my roomies had 911s of their own. I made a solemn promise to myself to turn my attention toward their priorities just as soon as I finished taking the upcoming LSAT. I spent the rest of the day studying, quizzing my roomies on their love lives and, of course, chatting with Olly.

Chapter Eighteen

That evening each of us brought up a plate to the rooftop deck. I had bought a monstrous caramel cheesecake from Eli's Cheesecake Company, my favorite. Meryl had made a large bowl of Greek salad, and Barbara was fighting Ella to carry the chicken cacciatore. "I'm not dead yet, dolly!" We could hear Barbara's voice coming up the stairwell. I couldn't help but laugh.

"Will someone get the door?" Ivy attempted to yell, holding her fleece blanket between her teeth. She had two bottles of red wine and cocktail mixers for Barbara.

Meryl turned on the fire pit. The heat blazed up. Ella turned on her iPod dock to Barbara's favorite playlist, *Hits from the 1950s,* and Ivy poured drinks. I popped a piece of some wonderful gouda in my mouth, washing it down with a red wine that tasted bitterly sweet. The wind was mingling the mix of perfumes we'd all been wearing that day: Barbara's rose-scent, my Coco Chanel, Meryl's sweet lavender, Ella's sugar vanilla, and Ivy's mystery scent that reminded me of mandarin oranges.

As we set up the plates, forks, knives, and the buffet-style dining, I watched Barbara glide across the roof in her embroidered coat with her matching scarf blowing in the wind. She truly was a free spirit, at times completely oblivious to the world around her. She twirled and faced me. "Bobbie, baby, did I ever finish telling you about the true meaning of love?

"Oh, the meaning of love..." I looked at the girls, smiling. "No, Barbara, please do finish telling us about the meaning of love!"

"So where did we leave off?" she asked as she twiddled her fingers, motioning Ivy to fix her a cocktail.

"You told me about Eros and Philia..."

"Ah yes, that's right, the passion of Eros, the enduring friendship of Philia. Dollies?" she called to Ivy and Ella. "Did I ever tell you two about the meaning of love? Meryl?"

Meryl shook her head no, Ella shook her head no, and Ivy began talking with food in her mouth. "Like only about a hundred ti—" She was cut short in mid-sentence when Ella discreetly kicked her.

"Oh, riiiight...the meaning of love," Ivy said. She looked at me, covering her mouth with her hand and whispering, "Only a hundred times."

I couldn't help but think that the meaning of love wasn't something you should hear just once.

"Eros is the spirit that inspires love between two people," Barbara said, as the wind dramatically whipped her scarf behind her. "You know, the butterflies. Now...Eros is quite cut and dry. Either you want to be stark naked under the sheets or you don't! Am I right, ladies?"

"That depends. How many drinks have I had?" Ivy asked.

"As long as he has a six pack!" Ella said.

"And, well endowed," I said scandalously.

"Bobbie!" Meryl exclaimed.

"Endowed with creative talent!" I corrected and smirked.

"Oh, she right's about that, honey," Barbara said and winked at us.

We all fell over in laughter.

Barbara sat down like a queen on a throne, and like devoted subjects, we gathered around her. Due jumped up on her lap, and she stroked him as she talked. "In the beginning," she said, "a person is always going to put their best foot forward, you know, the men showing off...the girls with their makeup and perfumes...But love takes time and patience. These two people must go through both joys and sorrows, pleasures and pains, and still in the end want to be together. Philia is the true test of the relationship!"

Barbara took a big swig of the cocktail Ivy had served her. Raising her finger, she said, "Last but not least, we have Agape. Agape is the fusion of Eros and Philia. It is much more difficult to comprehend and almost impossible to understand. The only way to understand Agape is to live it and let it consume you. Agape is unique for everyone, but it is truly what binds us."

Silence descended as Barbara paused, until a hint of wind rustled the dead leaves. The fire pit crackled in the background.

"Find a man or be found by a man, and be in love with his uniqueness."

Hanging onto every word out of Barbara's mouth, I began to feel my heart race, my head spin. I felt simultaneously lighter and fuller. *That's what this is,* I thought. *That's what I'm feeling.*

When I thought about Oliver, I realized he had an affect on me that no one else had. I couldn't explain it. I felt at home yet freer than ever. It felt natural yet thrilling. It felt solid and at the same time, light. It was all something foreign to me, something I had never felt before. I began to chuckle, tears filling up my eyes with joyous relief. The girls looked at me. I then began to laugh uncontrollably, tears streaming from my face, they looked at each other. Barbara gazed at me with a nod, she knew.

"Girls...I want to be naked with my best friend! It is the fusion of Eros with Philia. I found Agape!"

I held onto my chair because I thought I'd fly away, my head spinning.

I was in love.